PACIFIQUE

SARAH L. TAGGART

COACH HOUSE BOOKS, TORONTO

first edition

 Canada Council **Conseil des Arts**
for the Arts **du Canada**

 ONTARIO ARTS COUNCIL
CONSEIL DES ARTS DE L'ONTARIO
an Ontario government agency
un organisme du gouvernement de l'Ontario

Canadä

Published with the generous assistance of the Canada Council for the Arts and the
Ontario Arts Council. Coach House Books also acknowledges the support of the
Government of Canada through the Canada Book Fund and the Government of Ontario
through the Ontario Book Publishing Tax Credit.

LIBRARY AND ARCHIVES CANADA CATALOGUING IN PUBLICATION

Title: Pacifique / Sarah L. Taggart.
Names: Taggart, Sarah L., author.
Identifiers: Canadiana (print) 20220199442 | Canadiana (ebook) 20220199450 | ISBN
9781552454473 (softcover) | ISBN 9781770567320 (EPUB) | ISBN 9781770567337
(PDF)
Classification: LCC PS8639.A325 P33 2022 | DDC C813/.6—dc23

Pacifique is available as an ebook: ISBN 978 1 77056 732 0 (EPUB), 978 1 77056 733 7
(PDF)

This book is dedicated to my uncle
Douglas Murray (1948–2013), my advocate, my biggest fan,
and
to all the inmates – past, present, and future – of the
Eric Martin Pavilion and places like it.
May you find peace.

Prologue

Names for things come in fits. Light. No light. Light. Sky. Blue. The sky is blue. Sun. A twig at the corner of her vision. A branch. A tree. Overhead. A self, a body. Her. On her back, looking at the sky. Another twig. No. A pole, a metal pole, a street lamp. A street.

A man. Wearing dark blue. Navy. A uniform. A thick moustache, a mouthful of clean white teeth. And the eyes: determined, certain. Not friendly, not someone she knows. But safe.

'Oh shit oh shit.'

Words tumble out, an unfamiliar staccato in her ears. Then, other sounds. Mumbling. An engine rumbling. The smell of it. Diesel.

'Oh shit. Sorry.'

Not a cloud in that unending blue above her, just a slew of them in her brain. Where her brain should be. Real words don't come.

'Oh shit. Sorry. Sorry I'm swearing.'

Something. What. What happened?

'Be still, miss. You've had an accident.'

Gravity pulls on her as Moustache Man heaves. She's on a board. The board is rising into the air. A second person, unseen, lifts at her feet. A chill breeze tickles behind her ear. Into the rumbling van. An ambulance. Warm. Her temple hits the plastic encasing her head.

– thinking back later, she'll think she thought, *This is what dying feels like. Am I dying? Have I died?* Then she'll remember there was no thinking, no thoughts in her brain, her brain instead a cavern so big and so wide and so dark that nothing could get in or out of it –

Who. Where. Where is she?

'Where's Pacifique?'

They slide the board out from under her. She's on a stretcher in the back of the ambulance. The other uniformed entity comes into view, a woman, blond ponytail high and glossy, swinging like a child's.

Moustache fiddles with something out of sight. 'Pardon, sweetheart?'

'Pacifique. I was with Pacifique.'

Her lover. Her feet pressing pedals. A bicycle. Laughter behind her. Pacifique on another bike. The memory spirals into obscurity. She chases it. Everything above her neck starts to ache.

'Pacifique.'

'I'm sorry, dear, I'm not sure.' He looks across the stretcher at Ponytail. The van rocks as the paramedic steps onto the asphalt.

'I think you've got a broken bone in that shoulder,' says the man. 'You hit your head pretty good so I've got you immobilized. They'll X-ray you at the hospital.'

The words make sense individually, but the story is lost on her.

'You'll be all right,' he says, as if he understands her confusion. He pats her thigh –

– thinking back, she'll put a memory here: when she was six she broke her collarbone for the first time. She had barely started school, late summer, early frost on the big playground reserved for the upper grades. At recess, she fell. Off the slanting bridge, two squared-off two-by-fours glued together, two chains wrapped in thick plastic for handrails, the whole thing in retrospect an accident waiting to happen, and it did, she slipped and fell onto the bridge, stomach pressed into the cold wood, staring at the gravel below. *If I don't move, I'll be fine*, she thought, and she didn't move until she did, thanks to gravity, and hit the earth shoulder-neck first. She doesn't remember making contact or even the pain that happened after. Someone came to help, she doesn't remember who. Then she was in Mr. Carrot's office sitting on a hard wooden chair like they have in schools from the past, both arms straight at her sides, locked at the elbow, holding the bottom of the chair, the only way to pause the pain. Mr. Carrot's name wasn't Carrot, it was Kerrick, but with a name like that you were asking to be called Mr. Carrot and some kids couldn't pronounce names right anyway. She sat immobile and straight-armed until her mom came. She doesn't remember that part either, it could have been her dad, she doesn't remember the drive to the hospital, maybe it hurt too much. She does remember her father helping her dress in the mornings, the button-up shirts, each arm slowly guided through the sleeves, and then in reverse at bedtime, the stiff lying back in bed –

'I asked but no, nobody. Nobody else was here,' says a voice near her feet. Ponytail.

She jerks and doesn't get anywhere, everything strapped. She shrieks as a knife blade of pain rips through her shoulder.

'Careful!' Moustache lays an arm across her torso, pressing her back into the stretcher. 'You were alone, sweetheart. The person who called us, she says you were alone.'

Part 1

Chapter 1

They met in February. One day mid-month, after daffodils had already appeared on lawns, it grew cold. Colder than it had been in many winters. It rarely snowed in this temperate and coastal British Columbian city. People stayed home, scared of the ice and the wet snow that locked itself around car tires, weighed down power lines.

One Tuesday night the transformer at the corner of Tia's block blew. The light disappeared all at once and the power shut off with a soft *pop*. Surrounded by the sudden silence that comes with an outage, Tia chose not to dig out candles and instead ventured out into the hushed, frozen night. Her neighbours scurried about in their living rooms, huge shadow puppets huddled around kitchen tables set with small flames. She could barely make out the prints her shoes made in the snow, couldn't discern where sidewalk became boulevard, where boulevard became street. She looked for the moon. A sense of it blurred behind the tall maples that lined the road. It glowed small, a tiny crescent obscured by heavy clouds. Nothing to light the path ahead of her save for memory and, eventually, the rods in her eyes working overtime in the darkness. She didn't know where she was going. She was supposed to stay in, study massage therapy texts, memorize names: *scalene, trapezoid, pectoralis minor.* A body of fibres, sinew, and bone taking shape and making sense under her hands. She knew she wasn't dressed right, curled her toes in her sneakers against the numbness seeping in despite wool socks.

She was headed toward the ocean; in this part of Victoria, the sea encroached on three sides. She thought *frozen* even though the better part of her brain knew the harbour wouldn't flatten into a skating rink at a few degrees below zero.

Power returned sporadically after a few blocks. Street lights cast a hesitant glow that did not reach the sidewalk. Each one ringed by a halo of frozen air, a row of moon dogs parading down the street. The businesses below remained dark. Some restaurants were serving by candlelight. The few people exploring the streets were indiscernible. Tia looked for someone familiar, waiting for a smile she could return. Each face lay in shadow. She looked away and watched her step. Shivered.

She arrived at Bastion Square around eight. The square slanted on its journey toward Wharf Street, and the stones were slick. She slowed as she approached the stairs and the plaza below, where in the summer the man with the acoustic guitar played the same cover songs over and over. Tonight, it was empty. No music. Only the dim clatter of forks on plates from the Italian restaurant on the northwest corner of the square. Distracted, Tia squinted at the restaurant, wondering if they had electricity to cook pasta. The thought of warm noodles made her stomach grumble. She reached for the railing, found nothing, and slipped. The impact reverberated up her spine. Her skull tingled. Something about childhood spankings living forever in memory, the violation of being struck on the backside. Shame laced its rosy heat across her cheeks; disorientation threaded fog through her brain. She remembered the old woman who fell on these steps the summer before, the pattern of blood on her white hair. Tia reached for the back of her skull.

A hand in a white glove. Clear and bright in that otherwise fuzzy, gauzy space. A glove of creamy leather, mother-of-pearl buttons from base of thumb to wrist.

Tia would remember the buttons. This strange, snowy evening would become but a distant, dizzying dream and, weeks later, she would go searching for the gloves, quizzing shopkeepers, trying to find the store that sold them.

The woman wearing the glove kneeled and looked into Tia's face, her eyes wide and almost purple in the faded orange light of the square.

'Here,' she said. The r not a hard Canadian r, something softer, the word falling off at the end. She gestured with the outstretched hand

and Tia took it. She placed her other glove against Tia's lower back, a firm, unselfconscious pillar for Tia to lean against as she scrabbled to her feet.

She brushed snow from the backs of her legs with one hand and clutched the stranger's with the other.

The woman's bare head was piled with thick, dark curls, pinned at the crown and falling long over her shoulders and down her back. She wore all black: coat, stockings, heeled boots wholly impractical in this weather, although she was as solid on her feet as Tia wasn't. All black save for an ivory scarf – silk? – snug around her throat, and the gloves.

Tia tried to voice a *thank you*. A sly and invisible hand dipped into her jeans. A tickling along inner thigh, heat burgeoning between her legs. Her balance faltered, again. The woman would not look away. Her skin smooth and untouched, her age unknowable, cheeks lightly flushed. From cold? A suggestion of a smile twitched at one corner of the lipsticked mouth. Red like Okanagan cherries, the colour of a fresh bruise. Lids enhanced with liner – no, kohl, the edges smudged. One brow a boomerang, the eyes still fairy-tale purple in the obscurity of night.

Nothing about her *obscured*, Tia will recall later. Her face as well-lit as if she'd been standing in full moonlight.

'Let's get a drink. I know a place,' said the woman.

'Yes,' Tia said, before the woman's words were properly formed in the snow-speckled air.

'Do you need a hand with the stairs?'

Tia realized she'd fallen on the cobblestones leading to the steps. She hadn't even made it to the treacherous part.

'I think I do,' she said with a small laugh. Her solar plexus relaxed.

The stranger offered her glove and Tia took it. Heat leached into her fingers as if the leather flowed with the woman's own blood. Tia stole a glance from her companion to find the railing, and together they descended. The square echoed with their steps, Tia's breath, the rasp of her denimed thighs meeting, the sound of a heart pumping, fast like a train gathering speed.

She watched her feet cut a swath through the soggy snow, tunnel vision collapsing her world into a tiny space where only she and the stranger existed. She felt her hand grow hot in the mitt locked in the glove. The woman pulled left and they descended a dark staircase toward a soft neon glow blinking at the bottom.

The neon was a sign burning over a towering, sleek black door untouched by a doorknob, a window, or any markings. *Nightclub* blazed, on and off, in luminescent blue. Ahead, a sidewalk snaked along the side of the building. Several dozen people appeared to materialize on the pavement, waiting in line in the shadows. Tia stepped closer to her guide. They didn't join the queue; instead, the woman led her past the looming bouncer with a light wave of her white glove and pushed open the door.

Tia was pulled through the doorway. Darkness and the booming bass of electronic music fell over them like a shroud.

The plain exterior and small, hidden staircase belied a cavernous space. Tia felt like she was floating, surrounded by so much blackness. Ceilings at least thirty feet high, a catwalk along the perimeter. Dark walls, ceiling, floor, everything, as far as Tia could tell in the low, strobing light.

Why have I never been here? she wondered.

The woman put a gloved finger to her lips. With the same finger, she pointed to a trio of figures under spotlights. They stood on a raised platform at the far end of the club and wore period costumes – two women in gowns with generous bustles, a man in breeches. Tia caught snatches of their conversation as they approached. No, not a conversation, their lines. A play.

'A creature of the night, madam,' shouted the man over the music. His velvet pants fit snugly over lean glutes, bulky quadriceps. His forehead shone with sweat. 'A vampire. That is what I am.'

The women tittered.

Tia's companion looked over her shoulder. 'I've seen this one,' she said in a stage whisper, grinning wide. Her lipstick looked black in the steep shadow cast by the stage lights.

All of a sudden, Tia felt herself float away. She saw the woman's bright teeth, tinged purple by the black light, and the slightly stooped blond woman who was herself, the pair of them beautiful here in this moment. The grinning woman turned away, back to the play, and the dizzying moment passed. Tia was once again in her body, which tingled with nerves and moisture in the close, warm room.

'Sir, we're ignorant ladies,' said a woman onstage, stepping forward. 'We know not what a vampire is. A creature of the night. Won't you... show us?'

This time the audience tittered.

The second woman glided to her friend. The bustle of her periwinkle-blue dress bobbed behind her. 'Yes, won't you?'

A man in the audience let out a deep, rumbling chortle; the woman winked in his direction. The lights dropped. The spectators erupted in applause, a contagious enthusiasm. Tia brought two fingers to her mouth and whistled.

In the next moment, pounding bass returned to the quiet corner, dispersing the crowd. They milled around Tia, cutting her off from the person who'd brought her here. A woman with black-and-red dreads sprouting from her head like vines, a man wearing only pleather shorts and running shoes, a towering drag queen in four-inch heels. Her bare bicep brushed Tia's shoulder. Tia was startled by the damp heat of it.

The dark-haired stranger darted through the throng and grabbed Tia's mittened hand. 'That's one of my favourites. You'll have to see the whole thing sometime.'

She led Tia through the crowd into the opposite corner of the club, where a steep steel staircase better suited to a construction site climbed toward the catwalk. The steps shuddered, the rough surface digging into the soft soles of Tia's sneakers. The catwalk hovered some twenty feet above the dance floor. The din faded by a handful of decibels; the bodies below pulsed as a single entity, staccato in the flickering light.

The woman let go of Tia and, without a word, disappeared. Tia stopped, spun around. The catwalk leading back to the stairs was empty.

Had she fallen? Tia peered over the edge of the railing, then swiftly pulled back, the nausea of vertigo crawling up her throat. She turned around again. No one. Then, emerging from the wall, the white glove. Tia grabbed it.

The woman pulled her through a gap in the wall, a doorway, and then a curtain of heavy velvet. The music fell away into a distant, muted bass line. They stood in an empty, better-lit room. Persian rugs hung on the walls. The carpet was soft, plush, deep carmine. A black leather bench ran along the walls on all four sides.

'It's a bit of a silly room,' said the woman.

Yes, that was the word for it. Silly.

'But it's quiet.'

The woman, finally visible in the steadier light of the silly room, turned to Tia and took off her right glove.

'I'm Pacifique,' she said, holding out a hand.

'Pacifique,' Tia repeated, imagining the unending expanse of the ocean. She took the offered hand.

Pacifique held Tia's wrist and with her other hand removed the mitten. She pulled Tia's fingers to her mouth and pressed her lips to Tia's knuckles. Left them there for a moment.

Before she pulled away, something flashed, peeking under the edge of her scarf: bright white skin, mottled, where the neck curved into shoulder. Then gone. A trick of the light.

Let me take a look at you, Tia wanted to whisper. Should she? *Is this a date?* Tia didn't know what a date with a woman was supposed to feel like. She'd certainly never been on a date like this.

'Let's sit,' Tia suggested. As soon as she sat she regretted it; the leather benches proved firmer than they appeared and a lightning strike of pain travelled from coccyx to skull.

'You must have hit the ground pretty hard,' said Pacifique. That same soft smile played at the corner of her mouth.

At first glance, Pacifique was a beautiful woman. On second, maybe a shade too different to be beautiful. Stunning. The quality that gets you on movie screens, in magazines, makes people turn in the street. It wasn't just her face. It was that tiny figure, maybe five feet, though her spike heels made it hard to be sure, and those raven curls. A surprising constellation of orange freckles speckled her nose.

'I don't have an explanation for these,' Pacifique said. She brushed a fingertip, manicured nail painted royal purple, across her nose, her cheekbones.

'Where did you come from?' Tia asked. She felt fuzzy, almost shocked.

'You work with your hands. I can tell.' Pacifique played with Tia's fingers. 'You take care of these hands, too. They're strong yet soft.'

'Massage oil.'

Pacifique gave her a quizzical look.

'I'm a massage therapist,' Tia said. 'Well, training. I'm in school. All day, every day, I work with massage oil.' She'd told this story before, but everything she said to this woman seemed to carry extra weight. As if each syllable were being studied, examined. 'What about you? Are you an artist?' Something about the woman's style, her aura.

'Oh, a little bit of everything. I do a bit of everything.' Then, 'I'd like you to come home with me,' said the woman.

Tia swallowed hard against the quicksilver that rose in her chest.

'Mm-hm.'

'I'll cast your runes.'

Tia blinked.

'Don't worry,' said Pacifique. 'I'll show you.'

They stood and Tia turned to leave the room the way they'd come in.

Pacifique hooked her small fingers around Tia's wrist and pulled her in the opposite direction. 'There's a back way.'

She took her into the corner, which concealed another doorway. Beyond stood a heavy Emergency Exit door, the big red octagon blaring STOP. Pacifique pushed the bar, and the door clanged open. No alarm. Brisk sea air rushed through Tia's open collar. They stood on a fire escape more rickety than the staircase to the catwalk. The harbour spread out below, inky and wide open, wavering silver under filmy moonlight.

Another bolt of vertigo stabbed Tia's gut. Pacifique ignored the view and bounded down the steps as if she'd done so a dozen times.

The street that bordered the harbour ran white and silent with ankle-deep snow in both directions. Restaurants lay dark. The temperature had risen a few degrees in the hour – hours? – they had been in the club. Snow melted under their steps; the street lights no longer glowed with halos. Pacifique grasped her hand and squeezed. Night stretched ahead of them like a waterfall begging to be leapt. They saw no one. The night felt complete, folding into itself as happens very early in the morning.

Deep in James Bay, Victoria's oldest neighbourhood, they turned down a street Tia didn't know and walked to its end. They arrived at a large heritage house and climbed three flights of stairs to the top floor. Tia tried to unlatch her fingers; Pacifique held tight. She turned the doorknob with her free hand. Incense – sandalwood, patchouli – wafted out. And woodsmoke, as if a fire were burning. Pacifique reached around the frame, flicked a light switch. Inside, a cave of reds and golds, tapestries and swaths of fabric on the walls and covering most of the floor, the rich colours of India, China. Or African sunsets, colours Tia had never seen in a West Coast sky. The space was one big room lit by a single fixture in the middle of the ceiling, wrapped in a paper lantern. Books lined the room's baseboards, double-high. Semblance of a kitchen in the far corner. Bay window to Tia's right, overlooking the street. No curtains. In the corner opposite the kitchen, a bathtub. The only suggestion of a wall a folding panel shielding the tub. At the panel's base sat an aquarium, empty. And there, against the far wall, a small green metal stove the size of a banker's box, burning wood. It stood on a platform of slate tiles and its chimney rose through the ceiling and disappeared.

✳

'She left a fire burning?' the psychiatrist asks.

'It was smoking at that point. Embers, mostly.'

'You'd been out for hours. It was probably a healthy fire when she left. Would you leave a fire unattended in a one-hundred-year-old house?'

'Well, no. Unless I forgot. Maybe she forgot.'

Pacifique was not the kind of person to forget. She had left the fire burning for Tia. This isn't something she can explain to the doctor.

✻

Pacifique removed her woollen peacoat and hung it on a wrought-iron hook. She took Tia's down jacket, placed it on the next one. An errant goose feather floated to the hardwood floor. Pacifique unzipped and then kicked off her knee-high black leather boots. They skittered across the slick, shiny floorboards. Tia tucked her sneakers against the wall in the narrow space between door jamb and the first set of books – hardcovers, old. The once-white rubber toes of her Converse shoes were scorched black with grit and road tar, the canvas wet with snow. She grimaced.

'Don't worry about it,' Pacifique crooned, and pulled her into the middle of the apartment. She melted at the knees onto the rug below and snugged a pillow at her lower back. 'Sit,' she commanded. Tia did as she was told. From under the pillow, Pacifique pulled a dark-coloured bag, twilight bluish; it was hard to say in the reddish light. Everything was cast in crimson shadow. The pouch was made of soft leather and gathered at the neck with what looked like twine, suitable for tying boxes. Pacifique loosened the tie and handed it to Tia.

'How many?' Pacifique asked.

Tia stared.

'How many stones? One, three, or five?'

'Am I supposed to know?' The smile that pulled at Tia's mouth felt too wide for her face. She named the feeling spreading through her chest: happiness.

Pacifique waited, offering only a soft smile in return.

'Three?' Tia guessed.

'A pragmatist. Good.'

Tia felt pride despite herself, a child praised.

'Come,' Pacifique said. 'Close the circle. Create a safe space within which to throw the stones.'

Pacifique sat cross-legged, looking composed despite the tight-fitting skirt she wore. Tia scooted forward until the faded knees of her jeans touched Pacifique's stockings. With contact, a jagged nerve ignited from patella to hip to groin. She clenched her teeth. Tia's eye caught on the dark space under the woman's skirt, where her nyloned thighs met.

'Three runes: three eras. The past, the present, and the future,' said Pacifique. Again Tia noticed the rolling *rs*. And the delicate *ts*. 'Hold the bag. Send an intention into the stones.'

Tia frowned as she took the pouch. Hard, rectangular blocks played under her fingers. The runes clicked under the fabric, many more than three from the feel of them.

'Your intention can be a question, something you're wondering about or need guidance with. Your intention can be a goal, a hope, a dream. Or you can simply put your heart and soul into the care of the stones and let the stones tell you what they will.'

Tia cast about in her mind for a question, for some intention perfect for this occasion, and discovered that, for the first time in weeks, maybe months, the ever-present buzz had subsided. In her brain she found only space. A warm, soft space, not unlike the room she found itself in.

'Take your time. I'll make tea.' The fortune teller stood in one fluid motion, legs unfolding like an insect's wings, and turned on the balls of her feet.

Tia shut her eyes. A tap squeaked open and water whooshed into a pot. Leaves gusted against the bay window.

'When meditating, we watch the distractions come and we watch them go. We don't get attached,' said Pacifique from the corner of the apartment.

Tia kept her eyes closed, relaxed her cheeks, felt the line of concentration across her forehead spread and release.

'Be honest with the runes and they will provide.'

Tia had always carried anxiety, like a security blanket she knew she didn't need, knew didn't keep her safe from anything, yet couldn't shake. Her mother had told her once, after they'd had too many glasses of wine, that Tia didn't cry when she was born. Even when the needle punched her heel, her first blood sample, all she did was whimper. 'Scared of the world, you were,' her mother had told her. 'Right from the beginning.'

None of that now. Now, a sense of rightness in the world. *I am happy*, she thought, and imagined the words jumping from her brain into the bag of soothsaying stones.

※

'Nightclub? The place was called Nightclub?' her housemate and massage school classmate, Melissa, asks her later in hospital.

'I don't think it was really called Nightclub. I think that was just a sign they put up.' Early in her institutionalization, she still feels like things can be explained.

'There's nothing at the end of that block but an oyster bar.'

'They must have closed.'

'There was never anything there. Still. Jesus, Tia. You let a complete stranger take you to some unknown goth bar? Into a private room – a private sex room, probably!'

Tia snorts in response, then sighs. 'You would have gone, too. Anybody would have. This woman ...'

'I guess,' Melissa says. 'You noticed the colour of her *nail polish*?'

'I noticed everything.'

※

Not exactly true, she thinks, still later. She didn't notice the warning signs. Didn't notice, for example, that she and Pacifique spoke only twice about what Pacifique did in her spare time, something a doctor will be quick to point out.

'What did they say?' Andrew wonders when she tells him the story. One of the first questions he asks after meeting her in hospital.

'Who?' she says, playing dumb. 'What did who say?'

'The runes. What was your fortune?'

It is difficult to tell a lie in a mental hospital, to a fellow patient, a man who believes in visions. The drugs coursing through her system are stripping away inhibition after inhibition. A truth serum. She doesn't want to tell the truth. All she can muster is, 'I don't remember.'

Andrew frowns, then nods, two parts at once comprehending the game Tia is playing. He hasn't asked because he believes in fortune-telling. No, he believes in symbols and what our visions tell us about ourselves. Melissa, she knows, believes in none of these things. Friends new and old see her differently now. Why tell them anything, then?

✳

Why tell them that when she took the first sip of the tea Pacifique offered, she grimaced? The steam redolent of earth, like hay in a barn. Underneath that, something unmistakably sensual – a heady odour of chocolate and hashish, almost, although Tia hadn't smoked hash in years.

'It's kava kava. For your nerves,' Pacifique explained.

Years ago, a hippie friend of her mother's had suggested she take kava kava for anxiety, but Tia preferred the tiny pills prescribed by her family doctor. Everything in the world suddenly, magically manageable. A brief respite. She became addicted, not surprisingly. Who wouldn't, to a drug like that? The doctor refused to prescribe her more, and the anxiety, wrested from its drug-induced slumber, returned.

'Try some more,' Pacifique whispered. 'I made it weak, with some matcha to offset the sleepy effects.'

'My own personal herbalist,' Tia murmured, and put her lips to the cup once more.

'If you like.' Pacifique's fingers found the base of Tia's neck.

How to explain that when Pacifique cast the runes Tia had chosen, each told a highly improbable story?

'Your past is marked with neglect: your mother, your father, lovers. You are a giver, and you give more than you receive.'

Tia flushed with shame and dropped her face to look at the cup of tea in her hands. For a second, she resented the woman across from her. *How dare she know all of this?* There was something else there with the shame, though: a door in her chest opening, a soft glow of warmth taking purchase. The resentment flickered, then disappeared.

'The present: a person has come into your life. A woman. She speaks to something in you that you didn't know existed.'

Who would believe this was said in complete seriousness?

The final stone came to a rolling stop on the rug between them. Pacifique studied it, saying nothing. Finally: 'This is your future.' Another pause.

'Well?' A warm sip of tea curled into Tia's belly and worked its way through a knot. 'What does it say?'

'Tragedy. Tragedy is on its way. Something you love will be taken from you – or will disappear. It's unclear. You will suffer greatly for it.'

A nervous chuckle slipped from Tia's mouth.

'I'm sorry, Tia. I can't lie. Sometimes the runes tell us things we'd rather not hear.'

'It works out in the end, though, right? Happily ever after and all that.' A sliver had appeared in her voice. All of a sudden this didn't feel like fun.

'I can't see that. It's obscured.'

'Great!' Tia took one hand off her mug and rubbed the centre of her chest, pressing into the sternum until it hurt.

'We determine our own fate,' said Pacifique. 'The runes simply tell us what may happen. A possibility.'

Tia took a deep breath, feeling the hand there move up and then down.

'Let's put these away,' said Pacifique tersely. 'Drink your tea.'

How to tell Andrew, the doctors, her roommates, any of this? How to tell them that when moments later Pacifique put her lips to Tia's earlobe, a part of her felt like she was deliberately being distracted from the bad news foretold by the runes? How to tell them she didn't mind, couldn't mind, not when Pacifique's tongue went from earlobe, to neck, to shoulder. How to explain that Tia was first to offer her mouth, the one to take Pacifique's small palm and place it under her breast. The one to slip a hand beneath Pacifique's skirt and press it to the woman's crotch, then to struggle with the elastic waistband and reach beneath stockings, beneath panties. She wanted to take over Pacifique's body like an octopus stretching itself over coral. How unfair that she had but two hands.

✳

There is no way to explain this to any of them in hospital, to groups of people wracked with guilt over things done while insane. No way to satisfy their questions: *Are you gay? Did she seduce you? Were you high?*

She fights against having to explain. They ask because they don't know Pacifique. Don't know her energy, the aura she carries. A happiness people crave and rarely find. Pacifique offered her that happiness. Who would have said anything but yes?

Chapter 2

A madhouse is anything but mad. A madhouse is another system. System among systems. The ever-present chaos a distracting veneer. Underneath, pure order. A false order, yes, but order nonetheless. They want you to think it is a crazy place for crazy people. Andrew knows that every patient is just another cog in the machine. Like everyone on the outside. Inside, outside, it does not matter. *You're still a bloody pawn.*

＊

Most admissions come in by moonlight. He arrived that way. Policemen banging on the front door of his parents' home, dragging him through his mother's garden wearing a Manchester United jersey and a thinning pair of boxer shorts. They say he threatened his mother with a pair of her own sewing scissors. They say he was a danger to others and possibly himself. He has given up explaining that the woman he went after with the shears was not his mother. Their expressions glaze over; they have heard it all before. Do they not wonder why so many people coming through these doors tell a similar story? Of course not. They are members of the schema, mere cogs, operating under a pretense of power. *Doctor* a term they wear as if it means something, as if it frees them from the yoke of control. He is as daft as they are if he thinks he can break through their ignorance by raising his voice, presenting evidence. They do not want evidence; they want compliance.

So he complies. It is not so bad, being compliant. The drugs drag less and less on the corners of your brain. You gain a modicum of control over the insatiable hunger and the system with its unending food. Fattening you up, easier to control that way. You remember how to read, how to concentrate, how to think. Just be sure not to think too loud, because nothing is your own in this place.

Weeks back, Andrew would have been drugged and asleep in his four-bed room by now. After two months at the inaptly named Ian Charles *Pavilion*, however, the sleeping pills no longer throw him into slumber like they used to. If he wants to stay up, exert himself in a tiny way, he can. Tonight he does.

A madhouse measures sanity in decibels. A quiet patient becomes an invisible patient. Andrew tests the theory. He sits obscured in the dimmed ward in a chair he moved earlier in the evening from in front of the nurses' station to the edge of the cafeteria floor. Far from the nurses' hub without being exposed in the empty cafeteria space. A swath of moonlight cuts across his lap. A nurse from the neighbouring unit walks by, carrying an armful of board games. She does not glance his way. On her way back, arms freed of their cargo, she smiles the blank nurse's smile, does not stop. His silence is read as compliance.

The woman with the lank blond hair comes in by moonlight, via wheelchair. Not unusual. A brain on fire and a body debilitated – injured, withdrawing from street drugs, booze. An infirm mind creates an infirm body. Or the opposite: coked-out psychotics levitate off the squeaky hospital floor, their only gravity a security guard's fists around their biceps. He can't make out what the woman is saying, but he can hear the mania in her voice. She looks like a girl. Women and men reduced to children in this place. She slouches, hard lines of shoulder blades cutting through the back of her thin T-shirt. Andrew studies her figure: rapid weight loss. Happens. Her mania clearly long-standing, maybe months-long. The flesh on those bird-like upper arms jiggles as she gestures to the nurses behind the desk and the security guard at her back, telling them everything she has been telling everyone for weeks now. The same old stories, things they have all heard a dozen times. She obviously thinks she is telling them something new, something important. She must think she is here for a safe place to sleep. She displays no fear, only the ultimate confidence of the insane. She has no idea what she is in for. You start to understand how these things play out, what cog she will be.

The nurses ignore her and scuttle behind their desk: confirming meds, spelling of names, where to put her. They dismiss the guard. Before he veers left to the elevator, he spots Andrew.

'Hey, buddy. Whatcha doing?'

Andrew does not mind Lenny, one of the night guards, but they are not *buddies*. He would never deign to befriend a security guard. A man so indentured to the system he willingly participates in upholding its confines. Idiot.

Andrew watches the nurses. One of them has heard Lenny address him. Game over.

'Nothing, sir. Just chilling out before bed.'

He learned this, the mimicking of speech patterns to create intimacy, from a psychology textbook in university before he went proper crazy. The 'sir' is his own doing, a habit picked up at private school overseas and never dropped. That and the British accent. People respond well to both, so he uses them. He uncrosses his legs, signalling an intention to stand. Lenny has stopped a good two metres away. Assessing. Lenny and Andrew have been there and done that: Lenny held Andrew down on his second night while a nurse juiced him in the butt with several milligrams of lorazepam.

'Goodnight, Andrew,' says the man, firm and formal. A good security guard never assumes the best.

Andrew nods. He can play that game, too. This way he will be required to walk by the nurses' station, past the girl-patient.

As he comes up on the new inmate's right side, Andrew's nurse pops over to the corner of the station. 'Up late tonight, hey, Andrew? Do you need an extra zopiclone?'

He yawns. 'Oh, no, Sandee. No, no. Had real coffee today, from across the street. That was a mistake.' He measures the joviality in his tone. Too much and Sandee will come around from behind the desk, take his hand in both of hers, two fingers on his wrist and years of experience telling her how fast his heart is beating. He needs just a little, to ease her mind. 'I'll be off, then. Leave you to your charge.'

He sneaks a glance over his shoulder. The blond watches him. Circles the colour of ash underline each bloodshot blue eye. Her cheekbones stand out like cliffs in her hollow face. Andrew wonders when she last ate a proper meal. Psychosis-induced anorexia. Her crazy a list of symptoms Andrew checks off in his head.

She catches his eye and spits, 'Have you seen Pacifique?' The words topple into each other like dominoes.

'Sorry, who?' Sometimes it is fun to engage.

'Pacifique. Her name is Pacifique.'

'That's a beautiful name.' Once upon a time a woman named Beatrice lived in his head. She took care of him when his mother would not. He always thought Beatrice was the prettiest name.

The woman in the wheelchair smiles at his comment and opens her mouth to speak.

'But no. I'm sorry,' Andrew interrupts. 'I have not seen her.'

The woman's face collapses in on itself, a frightening metamorphosis of beauty – haggard, underfed beauty. He knows that look. That look of hate, of someone being dismissed. He has worn that look. Before she can respond with words as hideous as her expression, he turns and stalks toward his room at the end of the hall.

'You've seen her!' the woman shrieks at his retreating back. 'You have!'

He hears the high-pitched bark of rubber soles on hospital floor, a grunt of pain. He risks a look back. The woman lies on the ground. She tried to escape her chair, fell instead.

'Come on, Tia, let's not do that,' croons the head nurse.

Andrew perches in his doorway, watching. The woman, legs crumpled, spine twisted, arms bent in a push-up, scans the hall. She sees him. Spit sparkles on her chin. She swipes a rough hand across her mouth. Andrew closes his door, shuts out her unrelenting stare.

Into the dark room he shares with three other young men, now asleep and snoring through foggy, medicated dreams, he says, 'Welcome to the madhouse, Tia.'

Chapter 3

That first night with Pacifique, Tia had a dream. In it, she was playing
My Little Pony with a girl she had known in elementary school. The girl
had been an outcast, never had many friends, smelled of mothballs,
exotic cooking. She wore high-necked, lace-covered dresses with long
sleeves, and thick, bulky tights several sizes too big. They fell in folds at
her ankles, and Tia remembered wanting to hike them up for her, the
sight of them sagging over the girl's patent shoes like an itch she couldn't
scratch. Who knows what might have become of the girl – Nadia, Tia
remembered in the morning – if she hadn't drowned at a wave pool in
Vancouver. She'd been swimming with family and then all of a sudden
someone was screaming and she was lying on the bottom of the pool,
no telling how long she'd been there, the lifeguard unable to do anything
but breathe into her dead body until the paramedics showed up to do
the same.

Tia remembered the guilt she'd felt, as if her disdain for the girl's
upbringing, her culture, her clothes, had been responsible for her
death. The sense in the class that they should be sadder than they
were, but also that they were too sad, that it was unfair to expect them
to honour the passing of this girl no one liked. How to remember her
when they didn't even know her. The school assembly was a painful
hour of talks, a slideshow, one of Tia's classmates writing a poem. It
was Tia's introduction to death. A good one. Death was ugly and
uncomfortable and confusing.

In the dream, she and Nadia were adults. Nadia held a pony in each
hand, a boy and a girl, and she was forcing their rubber noses together.

'They're frenching,' she said to Tia.

Then she backed the girl pony up to the boy and put the boy pony's hooves on the pink backside of the girl pony. 'Now they're fucking,' said Nadia, and Tia giggled, nervous. Then Nadia dropped the ponies to the floor, a carpet made of coloured squares each containing a large digit, 1 through 9, like a rug you'd find in a kindergarten classroom.

'Now we fuck,' Nadia announced, and she leaned over and put her mouth on Tia's, her tongue an eel between Tia's lips.

Tia gasped awake, hand clenched between her thighs, fingers soaked with something thin and slightly gritty. In the bright sun of early morning she saw it. Blood. 'Shit.'

Pacifique stirred. The night rushed into Tia's brain, her groin. Pacifique. The woman with the violet eyes. Or – Tia turned to look, finally, in good light, but Pacifique appeared still deeply asleep, lids shut tight over whatever colour lay underneath. *Is she Persian, like Nadia?* Pacifique didn't sound like a Persian name.

✳

'Pacifique doesn't sound like a name at all,' Andrew says.

'You had an imaginary nanny named Beatrice walking around in your head,' Tia shoots back.

'Beatrice is a real name that people have.'

Pacifique. An odd name, sure, but the only name Tia can imagine her lover having.

✳

In the morning light, the strange woman slept. Tia slowly disentangled herself and hiked onto an elbow. She leaned in and craned to get a proper look at the cream-coloured mark on the left side of Pacifique's neck. It spread onto Pacifique's back and disappeared behind her shoulder. Even in the sunlight, she couldn't get a handle on it: A birthmark? An injury?

'You were dreaming.'

Pacifique's sweet, accented voice – was she Scottish? – sent a two-pronged shock through Tia's body. Desire and surprise, enough to make her jump. Caught. Spying. She swooped and planted a kiss on Pacifique's jawbone, one last study of the snowy map of the world taking purchase on her skin. Something on the skin, not a part of it. She pulled back, took in the morning face of the woman she had known only under nightfall. A band of sunlight like an arrow across the bridge of Pacifique's nose, cutting out whatever colour the irises might be.

'You were dreaming about a woman,' she said.

'A girl. She was a girl when I knew her. In the dream, she was a woman. My age.'

'A friend?'

'No. Closer to an enemy. Or the opposite of a friend, whatever you would call that.'

'We don't dream of people who are the opposite of friends.' A pause. 'It was a sexual dream.'

Something formal, stodgy, about the way Pacifique spoke. Tia snorted in spite of herself. With a look at the stained fingers draped over the sheet-covered figure, she remembered. A sharp turning in her abdomen, a need to urinate. 'Shit,' she said. 'My period. I'm sorry.'

'Oh, sweet Tia, don't worry.'

'Your sheets,' Tia protested. The ivory fabric covering them was softer and thicker than any bedclothes she had ever owned.

'I'll make a tapestry from the sheets you've bled on and buy new sheets.' Pacifique's voice rang high, an inventor who had stumbled upon her latest discovery.

From another creature the words would have sounded trite and weird, possibly creepy. A pump in Tia's groin told her she liked the idea.

'Yes, a tapestry,' she said again. 'To always remind me of this night.' Pacifique lifted her head, loosening the halo of black curls, and Tia moved to meet her. Before Tia could buck her hips out of reach, Pacifique's hand dove between her legs.

The sheet slipped away. Their bodies met in a way Tia never thought she'd know. A few sleepover pokes and prods as a preteen, pain and awkwardness the flavour of those moments. Nothing akin to this. Pacifique locked her hand between Tia's thighs, straddled her, a sprite on Tia's longer, meatier frame. That's when Tia spotted it, everything clear and brilliant in the morning sunshine, a tattoo planted between Pacifique's breasts and spreading under them and across the whole of her stomach. An animal. No, a creature of some kind. No, several. The picture disappeared as Pacifique pressed her torso to Tia's, and the moment of wondering evaporated with the flick of tongue against tongue and fingers come-hithering inside her, an ache of nausea and pleasure erupting when Pacifique found Tia's G spot.

In the hours that followed, the two women spent their time naked, wrapped in each other's damp limbs. Tia memorized the ink that decorated Pacifique's skin. She found the image at once grotesque and beautiful. She said so. Pacifique nodded. Whether it was acknowledgement or agreement, Tia could not be sure.

They didn't eat or sleep. When they needed sustenance, they drank tea, first hot, then whatever was cold and left on the counter. After night fell again, after the grit of various bodily fluids had infiltrated every fold of skin, Pacifique took Tia to the tub in the corner of the room. Infused the water with eucalyptus and something spicy Tia couldn't name. She told Tia to stand and, with the care of a conservationist bringing a classic painting back to life, ran wet hands between Tia's legs, combed through the light brown pubic hair, dipped tips of index and pointer between the lips. Tia's knees wobbled, and she grasped Pacifique's dark crown for support. She protested, mildly, when Pacifique replaced fingers with her mouth. When Tia came, she leaned into the arms of the woman kneeling beside the tub and watched viscous pink water dribble into her lover's hand.

The clock of their life together ticked over to twenty-four hours and kept ticking. Eventually, they slept.

*

'A chimera,' a psychiatrist tells her later, his Irish accent a touch like Pacifique's.

'What?'

'The tattoo. A creature with a lion's head, a goat's body, and a snake's tail? That's a chimera. Greek. A mythological creature. That is the typical iteration, but any combination of various mythical animals constitutes a chimera.'

Explain the magic away, Doctor.

'You never thought to ask Pacifique about her tattoo? Isn't that what young people do, talk about tattoos?'

How can someone so condescending work with crazy people?

'I told her it was beautiful,' Tia says, feeling stupid, duped, and caught at being stupid and duped. By a fucking wise-ass psychiatrist. 'I thought it was beautiful.'

Chapter 4

In line for lunch, Andrew sees her for the second time. The new girl. She wanders into the eating area. In the glare of near-noon sun and fluorescent lights, she looks worse than she did last night. Less high, too. The moxie sucked out of her like water drained from a swimming pool. Hair greasy and matted, bags under her eyes even deeper, spastic shuffle almost Parkinsonian. A mental patient if he has ever seen one. The nurses likely sent her over with vague instructions she cannot parse. Nothing makes sense in a madhouse at first. Stay long enough and you learn the system eventually.

'The lunch line is here,' he calls out.

She looks up, searching for a focal point and landing somewhere on his left shoulder.

'Here, the line. For food? Best to get in line now, if you want to eat.'

'Fuckin' starving,' she mumbles, words like jawbreakers in her mouth. Affectless. Doped right up.

'Here, go ahead of me.'

She shuffles in front of him, swaying a bit in her stockinged feet, one sock hanging long off the end of her foot like a flag. Bruce joins the line, dwarfing them both. If there are hard-boiled eggs on the menu, Bruce will take a dozen and will go back for seconds once the line has gone through once. He is a massive beefcake of rapidly dissolving muscle, well over six feet and wide like a linebacker. On his first day he claimed to be Bruce Lee, so that is what they call him.

At exactly 11:30 the wide door swooshes open and the new girl is not the only one shuffling, the line a caterpillar of crazies ambling to the beat of antipsychotics and sedatives.

She *is* starving: she takes four pieces – the maximum – of deep-fried fish and asks for another tongful of chips from the woman wearing the blue scrub cap. A disgusting ladle of tartar sauce later and she is ready to take her tray to a table. He attempts to grab her gaze as she shoves French fries into her mouth.

Forget that slag, mate. She doesn't remember you.

'Never mind,' he mumbles with a wave of his hand. The amnestic lorazepam she was riding last night probably wiped most of the previous day.

This catches her attention. Her chewing slows.

'Andrew. My name is Andrew.'

The woman grabs another chip and attempts to push it into the fray already in her mouth. 'Pffhtha,' she offers.

He stifles a chuckle. The woman snaps her head up. Her blue eyes drill into his like a raptor's. She becomes again the woman from last night, wearing the hardened glare of a person gone mad for too long and sick and tired of dealing with people who simply do not understand.

'I'm sorry,' he says, chagrined. 'I did not catch that. Your name.'

The blaze in her expression flickers out and is replaced with exhaustion. Twelve hours of sleep cannot wipe away weeks without. She breaks eye contact while she chews.

'Tia,' she says. 'I'm Tia.'

'Tia,' he repeats. 'Possibly of Greek origin? Thea was a Titan goddess, sometimes called Euryphaessa, and was said to be the mother of the sun and the moon. Right?'

He has held her attention another microsecond with this, but she is again suspicious. A glint of the raptor's gaze returns, and she says, 'Yeah. How'd you know that? Most people say, "You know that means *aunt* in Spanish, right?"'

Enthused, he replies, '*Andrew* means *crazy know-it-all* in Spanish.'

He clenches his jaw. Comedy does not always land in the loony bin.

She drops her head, grabs a piece of fish, and dunks one greasy end in the puddle of tartar at the edge of her plate. Before she shoves the cod in her mouth, one side of her mouth turns up.

Andrew's lips curl with a smile of their own, one of the only smiles to touch his face since he entered this place some two months earlier. A friend in the madhouse is the best friend you will ever have.

✳

That afternoon, he signs himself out to 'computer room' and journeys up three storeys to the computer lab that lies on the seventh floor, next to the locked geriatric ward. He and Riley joke that the patients here are one step closer, literally, to the afterlife. With his privileges he is allowed fifteen minutes once each weekday in the lab. He still cannot quite tell if it is paranoia, but he believes they monitor the computers and have the place fitted with cameras. He is almost always alone in the room, as he is today. The room's existence is not exactly advertised to the patients.

He sits down with the intention of emailing his mother. But she has not written to him and he was the last to write, so that task is over. He types 'Tia' into the search engine. He imagines what her last name might be. He comes up blank. Maybe something Swedish, for her blond hair, or solidly Scottish, for her complexion. He finds confirmation of what he said to her about her name but he forgot something: Thea was also mother to the dawn. His brain leaps to make connections – how she came in by moonlight, how they spoke first in sunlight, and how she has brought him what feels like a new day. A snicker erupts from one part of his brain and he grimaces, quick to close the browser, feeling all of a sudden surveilled. He returns to his email, refreshing and refreshing until he realizes he's five minutes overtime.

He runs out of the room and puts his hand in between the elevator doors to stop them closing. Inside, a frail man in a bright blue hospital gown and vivid yellow pants looks caught out. Andrew shrugs and half smiles, hoping to communicate *Do what you need to do, mate.* He does not bother to say anything. Whatever comes out of his mouth will not make it in its original condition to the man's brain. Part of Andrew wants to ride the elevator all the way down, get some real air, not the so-called fresh air of the roof garden. Wants to help this man escape. But he does not. He gets off on the fourth. Stands still and feels the door close behind him, shielding for a moment the man hiding behind him. Chances are that geriatric is already aware of the man's escape. Likely Lenny and the rest of the lemmings will be ready for him. Ready to take him down – with words, to start, especially because he is so old, but with force if necessary. Andrew cannot for the time being handle any more reminders of the confinement of this place. He thinks of Tia. If he is involved in helping an inmate escape, if he gets written up for being five minutes late, if he does anything wrong, he could find himself on step-down one floor below, locked up and overdrugged and away from Tia. No. He must be the good patient.

Christ, you've got it bad, don't you?

He cannot argue with that. The crush courses through his bloodstream. Craving another high, he steps into the sleepy mid-afternoon of the ward and goes to find her.

Chapter 5

Pacifique rode a pink cruiser with a black banana seat, black sparkling fenders, and pink and black handlebar streamers. The thing must have weighed a ton. Pacifique casually hiked it up stairs and left it unattended in the lobbies of shops and restaurants, never bothering to carry a lock or chain. Tia's bicycle had languished in the shed in the backyard of the house she shared with Melissa and Esther, a fashion student. When she and Pacifique wheeled it out on their second day together, it was clear it would need serious attention before it was rideable.

'Never mind,' said Pacifique. 'I'll bring my tools over and fix it.'

'Your ... tools? You fix bikes?'

'There's nothing a person can't do if she puts her mind to it.' She cast a long look beyond the roof of the shed to the pilot-light blue of the sky above them. 'Today, I double you.'

Tia swung a leg over the bike and perched on the banana seat. Her hands circled her captain's waist and her legs clamped the saddle. Pacifique pumped the flat pedals. She had dressed like a circus performer, or a burlesque dancer, a complete about-face from the sedate, almost corporate, outfit she had worn the night at the club. This getup was more in line with what the customers at Nightclub had worn: thick black leggings snug against hamstring and buttock, with a single white line up the back of each leg finished with a bow high on each thigh, like those old-fashioned seamed stockings; a hot pink leather jacket reminiscent of *Grease*; a pair of copper-and-black goggles that a scientist in a silent film might wear, or a fighter pilot; and the crowning piece – a pink-and-black tutu.

'A tutu,' says Andrew, incredulous.

Typically, he keeps his guffaws to himself. On the afternoon that Tia tells him about the first time she and Pacifique rode bikes together, however, the laugh bursts out like water through a broken dam.

'Your precious Pacifique was a ballerina, was she? My mum took me to *The Nutcracker* once. I think I saw her!'

Tia ignores him. Andrew – so staid, so conservative. She knows that the outfit sounds ridiculous, a sideshow costume not meant for public consumption. But the truth is that Pacifique pulled it off.

Doubling turned into a two-block-long adventure. Her sneaker caught in the back wheel of the cruiser, jolting both women forward. Pacifique, light on her feet like an acrobat, barely stumbled. Tia lost her grip on the banana seat and careened onto the pavement. Pacifique flung the bike aside and rushed over, tearing the knee of her skin-tight pants on the asphalt as she skidded to kneeling.

'Your head!' Pacifique reached out, as if to press Tia into the ground, as if to immobilize her.

'I'm fine. I didn't hit my head.' She peered at the flustered woman. 'Are you okay?'

As quick as she'd flown to Tia's side, Pacifique stood and turned her back. 'Let's forget doubling for today.' Her tone like that used by a tour guide to address a group of strangers. 'I want to see your house.'

'Oh, my house. It's nothing like yours.'

'No, that's not quite true. I want to see your bed.'

'My bed?'

'Your bed. With you in it.'

In her backyard, Tia opened the shed door, but Pacifique let her pink-and-black behemoth fall, fenders flashing, to the wet grass below and gathered Tia in an embrace that belied the delicate arms that made it. Tia's breath caught – from the severity of her lover's hug, from the lusting punch in her stomach, and from something new: embarrassment. Her neighbours might see. She squirmed.

'Shh, lover. There is nothing to be ashamed of.' Pacifique again in her head.

So they kissed like that, two women so closely bound they could have been one and, one shuffling step after another, they made their way to Tia's house, entered the back door, stumbled through the living room, and, in time, tumbled into Tia's bed.

※

Sometime that night – the time a flashing red 01:44 on the alarm clock, another power outage? – Tia woke alone. She listened for rustling in the house, heard it: water running in the bathroom. Then the whoosh and pipe-rattling that followed a toilet flushing in the century-old house. Creak of taps. Tia kicked out of bed, took to her feet, and then stumbled back, her centre of gravity gone, her head spinning. 'Whoa,' she said, voice rhythmic, like someone directing a horse. The spoken word disturbed the dark, moist air of the bedroom. She sat on the edge of the bed and breathed deeply, waiting for the new aroma of Pacifique to greet her nose. It didn't. The smell of sex was unmistakable, that heady mélange of sweat and cunt. Tia brought her right hand to her face. The skin leached the familiar tang of her juices. Tia wrapped the sheet around her shoulders and rose to greet her lover in the hallway. Instead, she was greeted by a shriek.

'Jesus, Tia, you scared me.'

In the dim, a frizz of tight curls caught the moonlight. Melissa ran a shuddering hand through her bedhead.

'Sorry,' Tia managed. And then, 'Have you seen Pa – have you seen my friend?'

'Who?' Irritation replaced Melissa's fright. Her moon face slowly came into view.

One eye shut tight against the wee hour, the other squinting.

Tia hadn't introduced Pacifique. Hadn't even seen her roommates since she met Pacifique. A thought jumped into her brain: what day was it?

'Where were you today anyway?' asked Melissa.

'Today.' Thursday.

'Class? I covered for you, told Sheri you were sick. I haven't seen you in two days. For all I knew, you *were* sick.'

'I was with a friend.'

'The friend you're looking for? Oh, crap, Tia, do you have some guy over?'

Melissa crossed her arms over her breasts, inadvertently pulling up the oversized T-shirt she wore, making it clear she wore nothing else. A spoon stirred in Tia's stomach. She glanced at the spot where T-shirt met upper thigh. Melissa stepped back, uncrossed her arms, and tugged the top over her buttocks.

'No, no,' Tia said, in part to herself. She liked Melissa fine, but the girl was terribly plain, and a bit boring. A perfect roommate, nothing more. 'It's a girl. A woman. A woman friend.'

'Oh, well, I haven't seen her. Look, I'm tired. We have class tomorrow. Your friend gonna be here still?' Melissa didn't wait for an answer. She padded into the darkness toward her bedroom, holding with both hands the hem of her shirt tight to the backs of her retreating thighs.

Tia found Pacifique curled in a ball in the centre of the bed. The covers a mountain toppling off the end of the bare mattress. The window at the head of the bed looked out onto the backyard and the moon, full, unclouded. In the colour-diffusing light from the moon, Tia studied the birthmark – or whatever it was, she had yet to ask – on the back of Pacifique's neck. She blinked away the dim. She tiptoed to the bed and crept, one knee at a time, onto the mattress. The mark skated farther than Tia had thought, one corner of the light-coloured blob reaching Pacifique's mid-back. It had no sense to it, no defined beginning or end. It was too dark in the room – Tia couldn't see. She put a hand out, leaned a few inches closer, and woke Pacifique.

'Come to bed, my beautiful Tia.'

Tia shimmied to meet her lover, who uncurled, turned over, and draped an arm and a leg across her.

'Where were you?' said Tia. 'Just now. I woke up and you weren't here.'

'I was probably dreaming,' said Pacifique.

That doesn't make sense, Tia thought, and would have said so – even though by then she had already figured out that not everything made sense when it came to Pacifique – but the naked woman wrapped around her had fallen asleep.

✳

'Does the psychiatrist have a hypothesis about Pacifique's birthmark, too?' Andrew, later. 'Perhaps it was the mark of Satan.'

Tia sighs. 'Pacifique told me herself. What it was. On our last day together.'

Andrew waits.

'Scleroderma.'

He doesn't have a smart retort to that.

'It's an autoimmune disorder. Chronic and sometimes progressive. I worried, when Pacifique – ' A pause. Searching, still, for a way to talk about the negative space Pacifique occupied. ' – went away, that maybe she'd gotten sick. Because the mark I saw on her skin, that thickening and contracting of the skin, it looked like armour, a shield. That's what the disease was doing on the inside, too. The skin stuff was a symptom of something much worse going on elsewhere.'

'Pacifique told you all this?'

'Yes. And I looked it up, afterward.' There were times before her arrest when she had considered, albeit momentarily, that she could be losing her mind. One afternoon she looked up the disease Pacifique had claimed to be suffering from. 'It all checked out, everything she said. Pictures, case studies.' Then, forceful, as if the thought has just occurred to her when in fact she's been harbouring it for weeks. 'That's weird, isn't it? I knew nothing about scleroderma before. Everything she told me matched exactly what I read about afterward. How could I have known any of that without Pacifique? Isn't that proof she's real? Was real?'

Grasping. Andrew won't be fooled.

'It is not proof, Tia,' he says after what seems to her an uncharitably short pause.

His voice isn't unkind, though. He isn't trying to be mean. He looks her square in the face and she doesn't look away.

'That is not what is important,' he goes on. 'Because a lot of what is most important to us cannot be proven or disproven.'

She doesn't know what he means.

As if he has read her thoughts, he says, 'You will have to find another way to make sense of this. Of her.'

Chapter 6

Tia becomes the typical mental patient: non-compliant. Compliance comes for everyone eventually – well, almost everyone – although some find it quicker than others. There are those who never comply, those who wind up incarcerated for life in one institution or another. Andrew did not find it right away. It is typically a longer ride for schizophrenics. Harder to find the right combination of meds, to get through the many layers of psychosis. *Depression has to be the worst.* One pill after another and the black, blank slate of the mind – the same black blankness every bloody morning. Compliance comes easily because why not? It's easy if you cannot even bring yourself to rise and open your mouth to take the pills tendered by the nurse, roll over and take a needle in the arse.

Tia's problem is Pacifique. The woman she claims was her lover (*didn't peg her for a lesbo*) disappeared after Tia went backside over teakettle on her bike. This information caught him off guard for several reasons; for one, he had assumed she was single. The accident happened a month ago, or two. Time a tunnel Tia cannot make sense of, the end closer and further away, the sides closing in and expanding. What does it matter, anyway, how long ago it was? Tia will be locked up for a while, maybe as long as Andrew, and by the time the doctors and nurses are done with her, she will want nothing to do with Pacifique.

And yet Andrew has to admit: the mysterious lover sounds compelling. His imaginary nanny, Beatrice, was a lovely woman, but she had a caboose on her big enough to push a train up a mountain, and a mole that looked like Italy growing on the side of her nose. Andrew has often wondered why his brain provided such an unattractive woman for his companionship. His mother's psychiatrist – who was, briefly and unprofessionally, his psychiatrist – suggested Beatrice was 'a counterpoint to your classically beautiful mother.' He did know Andrew's mother had a thing for cosmetic surgery, right?

Tia tells anyone who will listen about Pacifique, and even those who will not: Bruce, Lenny, Riley the failed physicist, the nurses, the men and women in scrub caps who serve them their breakfast, lunch, and supper. She takes up smoking – many patients do; it helps with the anxiety and is often the only way you are allowed off-ward – and tells the smokers on the roof garden about Pacifique. Within a matter of days, everyone is right tired of it. Even Tia grows quiet, enthusiasm dampened by the constant, inevitable refrain of 'No, sorry, I haven't seen her.'

At lunch one day, a new patient whose name Andrew does not know slams her tray down at what Andrew has begun to call, despite his knowing better, *our table*. Irritation floods through him and he is about to blurt out something unkind when Tia says, 'Pacifique. My friend. I wonder, I wonder, I wonder – ' The excitement is too much for her. She cannot even get the words out. Andrew slumps over his food – shepherd's pie, the gravy congealing as he stares at it. The new patient does not make any sign of having heard Tia.

From the table behind them, Jake, the former postie, says, 'She ain't real, girl. Move on.' Jake appears to have lost his patience with Tia (or knows better, knows that it is not worth his time to humour a crazy).

She blushes and her eyes well up. She begins to cry into her moussaka, the day's vegetarian option. 'But, but, but,' she says softly to herself. The zeal, the anger, are gone. And in their place, tears.

Andrew sees in Tia a flicker of another self, knows she has the ability to dismiss Pacifique. But she refuses. He knows that she hurts only herself, dragging it out like this. She will give up the ghost eventually. In the meantime, he will wait. He will talk to her about music, politics, and philosophy. He will show her how to make the best of the loony jail, this shared time.

Chapter 7

The bedroom was full of light, the bed once again empty. Tia shot up, sleep left behind on the pillow, her brain wide awake and buzzing with the familiar anxiety. As a girl, she'd had night terrors. These were different from nightmares, she'd been told by a child psychologist, a kind and cartoonish-looking man with toe-curling halitosis. Tia called him Ira because he reminded her of the Sendak character. She always felt better after seeing him, but the night terrors persisted. A massive metallic mouth-creature, all teeth, descending from the sky to swallow her whole. Or the tornado that spun when part of her brain knew she was awake, her mother shaking her, putting her in the bath. She quit going to the counsellor – 'Can you believe what that man charges?' her mother exclaimed one evening, poring over bank statements – and, one day, the terrors stopped. A childhood phase outgrown, as Ira said would likely happen. He never told her what might be wrong. She suspected he had theories, theories he kept for the private meetings with her parents.

In the terrors' stead: fear. An image displayed on the backs of eyelids shut tight. Fear became the first emotion she encountered when doing anything new. It didn't matter what it was – small talk in grocery stores, first dates, learning to drive, applying for massage school. A litany of physical symptoms to go with it: nausea, tachycardia, irritable bowel syndrome, insomnia. It was amazing what a person could get used to. Tia barely noticed anymore.

She noticed it that morning, though, in bed. The first time in a while that she'd felt it. Fear.

Where's Pacifique?

She pushed herself to the edge of the mattress and landed on something: a note under her palm. The script tight, small, beautifully legible.

Dearest Tia,
I have gone on a treasure hunt. I will find you. Have a good day at
school.
Love, Pacifique
p.s. You are a light, the sun.

First: *love*. One erratic heartbeat on top of another. Breath shallow, a blazing ball of heat in her stomach. Second: *school*.

'Shit, shit, shit,' Tia muttered, searching for the alarm clock. Discovered it under discarded bedclothes. *Late, late, late.* But she would go, if only because Pacifique wanted her to.

＊

School flew by in one long daydream. It would be one of the last days Tia went to class.

Afterward, on the front steps of the old courthouse where they took classes, Melissa caught her by the arm. 'You okay?'

Tia blinked, the reality of her roommate in front of her replacing thoughts of Pacifique. 'Hm?'

'Late, first of all,' said Melissa. 'And then stuck on Pluto for the rest of the day. Is it flu?' In a tone meant to sound casual, she added, 'Body adjusting to new germs?'

Tia didn't answer. The woman she'd been on Pluto with all day appeared at the base of the limestone steps, flanked by two bikes, one the black-and-pink cruiser, one unfamiliar. Tia skipped down the stairs to meet Pacifique, leaving a baffled Melissa in her wake.

＊

Melissa would be the one, two weeks later, to tell Tia she was at risk of being kicked out of the program due to truancy, that the instructor would leave no more messages on her phone. And, later, the one to fish the letter from the college out of the mailbox and say, 'Open it. You've been expelled.'

Each time Tia would say, 'I can't go. I can't. I have to find Pacifique.' In response to yet another blank look from Melissa, she would add, 'The woman who picked me up from school that day, with the bikes. And she stayed over. At our house.'

'I've told you, Tia, I have no idea who you're talking about.'

Fists balled at her sides, toes clenched in her shoes, rage swimming in the front of her skull. Never one to hit, never, never, and yet –

What good would it do? a soft, sane voice would whisper in those final weeks before she was arrested and taken to the emergency room. *What good?*

※

Outside the massage school, Pacifique leaned over the new bike and kissed Tia. In turn, Tia surprised herself by offering her tongue to the woman's open mouth. She stepped forward, hips pressing against the bicycle frame, arms wrapped around the shorter woman's shoulders.

Pacifique pulled back. 'This is for you.' She gestured at the bike.

'It's gorgeous. But no. What do you mean, for me?'

'It's a perfect bicycle for you: the comfort of a cruiser but fast. You'll have no trouble keeping up with me.'

Tia will remember that Pacifique said this with a glittering smile. Tia doesn't smile back, knowing somehow even then that she will never be able to keep up. 'Where did you get it?'

The ride was a sparkling mantis green, metallic paint luminescent in the sun. Tia looked up to yet another cloudless sky. She couldn't remember a February this beautiful, this clear. She turned her attention to the bicycle, bit the inside of her cheek. She didn't know much about bikes, but she could tell this one hadn't come cheap. The wheels were slim, the rims black and made of a material she didn't know. Fibreglass? It melded the properties of Pacifique's cruiser with the sleek lines of the bikes she had watched zip around the Olympic velodrome. She'd never seen anything like it.

Pacifique let her admire the present – and didn't answer Tia's question.

'No, really, I can't accept this. This must have cost a fortune.' What a fortune might be to Pacifique, she didn't know.

'You must accept it!' Hurt twinged in Pacifique's blue-violet eyes. Tia couldn't deny it: the woman had purple irises. 'I saw it and I knew you had to have it.' Pacifique paused and, looking down, ran a hand over the crossbar of her offering. Softly: 'Please take it.'

The words stumbled out of Tia's mouth before she had time to process them. 'Yes. Of course. I'll take it. I'll gladly take it.'

She wished, only a handful of days later, that she hadn't. That she had pressed Pacifique for an honest answer to her question.

✳

'Do you think she stole the bicycle?' Dr. O'Shea asks her on the ward.

'It occurred to me. Even occurred to me at the time, actually. She could have. I don't know.'

The doctor lets her ruminate.

'Thing is, Pacifique didn't operate within the rules of society. If I had accused her of stealing, she probably would have had some explanation for how what she'd done wasn't stealing. And if I'd managed to get her to admit how much she'd paid for it, if she did in fact pay anything, she would have wiggled out of explaining that, too, saying without saying that she had the money to pay for it.'

She struggles with what she means to say. Asking Pacifique about pedestrian things like money or the lawful ownership of property would have been like asking a wood sprite about the stock market.

'If the bike was stolen, and you suspected her of theft, and accepted the gift all the same, that makes you a type of accessory, Tia.'

Clearly this doctor has never met someone like Pacifique, because if he had, he'd understand that sometimes you don't give a fuck about stuff like that. Tia suspects that if she discussed Pacifique with her childhood psychologist, the man who understood dreams, the stuff of nightmares, he'd make some sense of this. He would know that even if it were a dream, it meant something.

To the uncomprehending doctor, Tia whispers what she remembers of a line she read in one of the many books that lined the baseboards of Pacifique's apartment. 'There are more things in Heaven and Earth than are dreamt of in your philosophy.'

Barely a fracture in the psychiatrist's poker face. Barely a hint that he has heard, that what she said, holds any meaning at all.

✳

One day, Pacifique pulled her bicycle off Johnson Street and rode a few metres down the sidewalk until she arrived at the door of a closed café. She waited for Tia to catch up, then, using keys, opened the deadbolt.

Tia was confused. 'You work here?'

'I used to.'

'The keys – '

'I'll return them eventually.'

A soft twitter of anxiety bubbled in her stomach. She ignored it and, holding the door with one hand and pushing her bike with the other, followed Pacifique into the shop. She lay her bicycle against the wall and turned back to lock the door behind them.

Pacifique was already at the espresso machine. She disappeared completely behind it, her presence given away by the familiar steamy, banging sounds that surrounded all espresso machines. Tia walked around to find Pacifique putting a small porcelain cup under a double-fauceted spout moments before it began to spurt liquid the colour of jojoba seeds.

'I'm going to guess you'd like a cortado.'

Tia laughed. 'Except I don't know what that is.'

'No, not quite a cortado. Something special.' While the espresso continued to pour, Pacifique leaned down to rummage in the fridge under the counter. 'Perfect. Go take a seat, my love. I shall deliver to your table.'

My love.

A few moments later, Tia heard milk being heated; moments after that, Pacifique was once again beside her. She set the coffee down on the table. 'It's a little like a baby latte, a cortado. But this isn't quite that. Try it.'

'I'll ruin the – ' Tia paused, trying to find a way to describe the art in the foam. 'Is that the moon?'

'Oh, you recognize it! Lovely, Tia. Yes, the moon from our first night together, and that's the harbour.' She pointed at what Tia recognized as water across the base of the cup. 'You must ruin it, or else you can't enjoy the drink I made just for you.'

Tia pressed her mouth to the edge of the coffee, the milky picture disappearing as she softly, carefully sipped. The milk warmed her mouth, the perfect temperature. She sucked back half of the cup in one go.

'It tastes like coffee ice cream.'

'Not sour at all? I wasn't a hundred per cent certain on my extraction.'

'Sour?' Tia couldn't remember any coffee ever tasting sour. 'No, it's incredible.'

'I knew it: your coffee is a cortadito made with cream.'

✳

The shrink pulled this apart, too, of course. First, 'Oh, so she worked a job. Or had worked one. And kept the keys after her employment ended, which raises further ethical issues.'

'Yes,' Tia says, jaw clenched.

Then, 'Which café on Johnson?'

'I don't remember the name. It was on Lower Johnson.'

'So somewhere between Wharf and Douglas.'

'Exactly.'

O'Shea pauses for a moment, counting on his fingers. 'Four.'

'Four?' Irritation starts to rise in her chest.

'Cafés. I can think of four cafés in that stretch.'

So fucking what? she wants to scream.

'Regardless,' he says, 'I'm hearing a lot of coffee and tea and exercise. Not a lot of food or sleep. Do you think that perhaps days of this could have contributed to the psychotic symptoms?'

How can he say in the same breath that he believes she was up all night and yet doesn't believe who she was with? Doesn't he see the hypocrisy? 'You can't pick and choose like that,' she blurts out.

'What do you mean, Tia? What am I picking and choosing?' He's writing notes again. He's classifying, deciding, minimizing.

She huffs. 'Never mind.' She stares at him with a look she hopes is stony.

In reply, he gathers his papers together and stands. An unusual brusqueness. 'See you in a few days.'

'Wait, what? A few days?' They've been seeing each other every other day.

'You're not the only patient here, Tia,' he says.

She wishes he would stop saying her name. 'I know that. I didn't mean to suggest I was.' She struggles to hold on to her anger but it dissipates. In its place: guilt, like she's done something wrong.

'We need to start weaning you off these regular appointments. Might as well start now.'

He's just one more person who doesn't believe. *Join the club*, she thinks. *Nobody believes.* If it weren't for the meds, she'd cry, bang her fists.

The Irish shrink doesn't bother nodding goodbye. He turns away and heads toward the psychiatrists' hallway. Before he rounds the corner, he says, 'Don't worry, it's a good thing,' and disappears out of sight.

Chapter 8

What are you in for? is not an appropriate question on the ward. However, it is considered impolite to resist when a patient wants to share. In time, as Andrew grows more comfortable with Tia, as the edge she rode in on softens, he tells her why he is there. Eventually. A story told by a schizophrenic is a story told in tangents.

Tia is new to the system and probably thinks this is a one-shot incarceration, that once she is out of here, she will never come back. He hates to break that spell when he tells her this is his third hospitalization. Like the Chronics in Kesey's cuckoo's nest, they are stuck here for life. Sure, she will get out (and so will he). Decertified and discharged and sent on her way. Sure, she will go back to a job or school, whatever makes up her *life*. She will be stamped WELL. But she will never leave this place. It sticks with you, occupies space in the limbic brain, a part of you that second-guesses every bloody move. *Am I crazy?* a constant refrain. Crazy not something you grow out of. He knows his own diagnosis will cling to him as long as he walks this earth. Sometimes, like this last time and the two before that, it will get the better of him. Tia does not realize this. Tia still thinks she is different, that all of this is temporary, a setback, an obstacle on the ultimate path to finding Pacifique. In that way, she is no different from other new patients. Each crazy thinking her crazy is special, when it is all just a variation on a theme.

If more people saw the truth Andrew sees, the system would fall. The system survives because it operates on the backs of so many millions of minions. For now, the system and Tia's unwilling place in it do not matter. The days and weeks pass and the system comes to mean less and less. He thinks more often as a minion might and he comes to find no problem with thinking this way. Reality has a way of reclaiming its victims. Should he go back to school? Could he be an electrician's apprentice after all? Could he love somebody, somebody like Tia, have a family? No, probably not, but it is nice to dream. A dream that normal people dream.

※

After lunch one day about two weeks after Tia's admission, they sit in the cafeteria and watch Stu, another patient, attempt to flirt with the latest female on-ward by teaching her how to play chess. The woman – barely a woman, she looks maybe eighteen – is not interested in Stu or chess, can barely wrap her muddled brain around what has happened to her and where she has landed, let alone feel comfortable enough to make a new friend. The girl scratches the stubble on her tiny shaved head – not as a signal, as Stu takes it, that she is thinking about her next move, but more an indication, judging by the look of her, that she needs a bath.

Tia interrupts Andrew's observations and asks him about his mother. His focus breaks and recalibrates on the patient at his side. Tia wears hospital-issued pyjamas. Andrew does not. He wears new jeans and a plain T-shirt. His mother noted his expanding waistline one day with a combination of disdain and excitement. On one hand, she now had a fat son. On the other, he needed her, if only for a spot of shopping.

Some mornings, he feels like an intruder. He feels further from crazy than he has in a long time. He is not long for this place. Ever since Tia flew in, though, he does not much want to leave. Upon the urgings of Tia's mother, a woman Andrew did not meet because he was out on a day pass with his parents, Tia bathed. His day pass was hardly that, just a couple of hours to have a meal on the outside, a gyro from the place down the block. He tried and failed not to stuff his face while Shirley, his mother, picked at a Greek salad, his father oblivious and buried in the newspaper. When he returned, he saw that Tia had washed the grease from her hair, which, Andrew had noted on Tia's second day, had been dyed blond. This reminded him of Shirley even though he knew this was ludicrous. Women dye their hair all the time. In all other respects, the two women are nothing alike. Tia soft where his mother is hard; Tia natural where his mother is fake. Tia pretty; his mother surgically so.

His feelings for his mother occupy their own place in his heart, or some organ where in the Middle Ages they believed humours resided, like his spleen. A hidden corner deep in his knitted parts capable of sheltering two opposite elements at once: love and hate. As a young woman, his mother had wanted children and loved him with an intensity that suffocated him as a boy. Her love was the kind he imagines one might have for a pet or a fur stole. Every time a piece of his psyche flakes off, a new chink appears in her perfect-mother exterior. A sin against her. If *stigma* comes from the word *stigmata*, Shirley Purser acts like it is Andrew who has driven in the nails.

He says none of this to Tia.

Instead: 'My mother is the reason I'm in here.'

Parents the perfect upkeepers of the system. Thinking their roles as guardians demonstrate love, concern. In fact, they simply make it easier for the other guardians – the doctors, the lawmen – to do their jobs.

'Why?' Tia asks.

'She called the police.' How many adult children in this ward are here because a mother or a father called 911? He guesses at least half.

This part Tia knows. It came out earlier in the week. 'I mean, why did she call them?'

Andrew could tell her. Tell her about the sewing scissors, the look of pure horror on his mother's face, which in retrospect was an expression not unlike pure joy, the face open, unfettered by gratuitous brain activity. About the police dragging him through his mother's garden. He chose to lie, instead, chose to hope that he would never again be that man.

The system yells from one side of his brain. He will never escape his fate as a madman. To pretend he will never again be that sick is only to pretend it will not return in double force. The other side whispers softer, telling him he is still a man burdened with free will.

'I'm sorry,' Tia blurts, interrupting the cerebral battle, 'it must have been awful. I'm sorry for asking.'

'Shirley was worried,' he says. 'She thought I might be in danger.'

'That's sweet,' Tia tries. 'In a way. I mean, I'm sure she meant well.'

Tia gestures, a gesture that captures the whole ward, their whole existence in that moment, two crazy people in a psychiatric facility in the middle of a small coastal city. A gesture meant to suggest no one would knowingly subject their child to this place, it all must have been a great misunderstanding.

The lie falls from his lips like a gift. 'I am sure she did.' Then Andrew gestures in return. He means to encompass three things: himself, Tia, and the two of them together.

Shirley knew, he wants to tell her, what a 911 call meant for a diagnosed schizophrenic. This is exactly what she intended.

'My mother's a bitch.' Tia punctures Andrew's moment. 'She has no idea what to do with me in here.'

The tone of her voice is so certain, so sure. A small part of Andrew flinches, the part of him that wants to believe in only good things about her.

'Most people don't,' he whispers.

'Yeah, but she's my mother! She's supposed to love me and worry about me, no matter what. If I'd broken my leg, she wouldn't rush out of here ten minutes after arriving, she wouldn't keep my whereabouts from my grandparents.'

'Do you want your grandparents to know where you are?'

That stumps her for a handful of seconds. 'I don't want them to worry. Everything's fine, I'm fine, everything's going to be okay, she could tell them that.' A pause. 'Even if she doesn't believe it.'

Andrew does not fill the space that opens between them, full of silence and other things he cannot name. She does not understand and that is okay. She does not know any better. He will show her.

'Shit, did Sharon really call 911?' Tia's voice bursts uninvited through the silence. 'At least my mom didn't do that.'

A door somewhere in his chest closes. 'Shirley.'

'What?' Tia says.

She is already a million miles away, attention caught by a patient on the other side of the ward. Andrew another distraction in a stream of endless distractions, people like presents she gets to open and then discard. In this moment, he has proven himself uninteresting.

'Shirley. My mother's name is Shirley.'

'Riley!' Tia shouts.

She ejects from her seat. She still has these spurts of mania that break through the meds. She might for a while. Each one carefully noted by her nurse. Each night the meds upped, changed, reordered, each day a new psychotropic carnival ride. Each day a new adventure, and another opportunity for Andrew to get through to her. She might not even remember this conversation tomorrow.

'Riley, how goes the atom bomb?' she says to the short, bespectacled man who stands on the lip where thin, commercial-grade carpet meets the linoleum of the eating area.

Riley's attention flickers to Andrew's feet planted on the shiny floor. *That's right, you bastard, you're reading this right.* In his life as a painfully shy and awkward science student, Riley has likely never had the opportunity to speak to a pretty girl. In hospital, all boundaries blur. Riley has become the man he has always wanted to be: a nuclear physicist. He introduced himself as 'Doctor' when he first met Tia. She came to Andrew afterward and said, 'Can you believe they committed a fucking doctor? I mean, he's in, like, quantum mechanics or something. You don't want to mess with a guy like that.'

Andrew said nothing. The truth will come out. Tia will forgive Riley, as Andrew did.

'Oh, oh, oh, oh, what's it called, noooooo … '

Andrew cringes. Sometimes Riley is impossible to talk to, his verbal tic so strong that heavy-duty drugs have not erased it.

'I had nothing, um, what's it called, to do with that.'

Tia laughs as if Riley has said something genuinely funny. Andrew feels a sneer riding a wave from one part of his brain to another. It does not make it to his face, and for this he is grateful. When he is well, he smiles easily, laughs well. Never let others know what upsets you. It gives them power over you. Add this tack to the affect-stealing drugs and he becomes a perfect automaton. Except where Tia is concerned, it seems. In another situation, he would not have felt like sneering. He would have thought, *I understand how this situation might lead me to sneer, but I do not feel like sneering right now*. Editor upon editor, pill upon pill, psychosis upon sanity, all piling up in his brain. This is supposed to be him getting better. He shakes his head and Dr. Riley glances over again. Let Riley think the head shake is for him. In a way, it is.

'Uh-ummm – ' Riley clears his throat. 'At least a decade before the first test in 1945, scientists in Europe were trying to split the atom. The Manhattan Project itself didn't officially launch until the United States got involved in the war.' Get Riley on a roll and the tic, the bad jokes, disappear, and a lecture takes their place. 'A lot of those scientists didn't even know what they were working on. They didn't see what nuclear fission meant, could mean. Einstein, he had an idea. The others, no. They didn't find out until after. At least, that's what they say. That information was classified for so long, it's hard to know what really happened.'

Andrew glances at Tia, who stares at Riley, rapt.

'Um, what's it called, what I mean is that was a long time ago. I wasn't even born yet.'

Another flimsy line and yet Tia laughs, an overzealous cackle. Riley beams, a spontaneous and entirely certain smile spreading across his face. A brief shot of confidence. Pride that he could be the one to attract Tia. She is a kitten greedily accepting a bowl of milk – it matters not who provides it.

Riley's smile fades. 'I'm not that kind of scientist. I wouldn't do that kind of work.'

Tia's face fills with what Andrew guesses is sympathy. She leans toward Riley, hand outstretched, says, 'I'm sorry. Didn't mean to joke.'

What is shocking is that Riley lets her hand fall on his arm and twitches only slightly, stays in place for a second, another, before stepping out of reach.

'*Disgusting.*' Andrew says the word to himself and, horribly, out loud.

Tia's eyes narrow on him for the first time in days, but the narrowing can't hide something new: hurt. And something else. Something familiar. A look he has seen before, a look he knows well, too. Fear.

Fuck. Gears clank in his brain. He grasps the pieces inside his skull that have fallen outside their carefully drawn lines, shifts into first gear, and zooms ahead.

Move past, move forward, don't get hung up on the accidents, mate.

'Excuse me,' he says as he leaves, voice clear, respectful, and resplendent in the heavier Manchester accent.

He tries not to hear Tia's laughter tinkling behind him, Andrew forgotten already, nothing worth paying

any attention to in this place 'cept that fucking pathological liar of a schizophrenic. That bastard cunt ain't even got a bachelor's, let alone a bloody PhD.

Thinks he can get in Tia's knickers if he tells her he's a doctor

a nuclear fucking physicist, thinks someone like her'd *give* him *the time of day if she weren't forced to, them both locked up*

in 'ere and nothing to do every day 'cept listen to a deluded piece of shit talk about atom bombs.

A fumbling, deluded piece of shit.

His brain stutters, stalls and starts, too much going outside the lines, this familiar anger for so many weeks a memory, distant. He let himself be tricked into thinking it was a memory when it is clear that none of this went anywhere, it was always sitting nearby in a dark corner, behind a loosely shut door. Waiting. Riley and Tia aren't the disgusting ones,

I am. I'm the fucking failure. Worse than any bad name anyone ever gave me. I don't deserve nothing but this place and all the lying, disloyal miscreants in it.

He makes it to the nurses' station. Manages to ask for lorazepam. Nurse hands over a paper cup containing one tiny green pill. He risks a moment of eye contact and curls his fingers to indicate he wants more.

'How much?' she asks.

'Two milligrams.' Pushing, grinding the gears. 'Please.'

The nurse gives him a look. He knows he'll be talking to his psychiatrist about this tomorrow. Right now none of that matters. What matters is getting past this, forgetting, if only briefly, how locked he feels right now, how trapped. *Feeble-minded*, they used to call people like him. *For good reason.* The nurse replaces one cup with another. He takes the larger pill between thumb and forefinger, opens his mouth, and places the blue oblong under his tongue. A rush of calm, release. Help is on the way.

Chapter 9

Whoever built Tia's new bike built it for speed. Tia pulled ahead several times during their first ride together, which took them from the late afternoon into the darkest hours of the night. The city shrank under their tires.

After night fell, they sped along a slick residential street, past darkened neighbourhood grocery stores and more closed coffee shops, straight to the sea. A path of light snuck under Tia's tires, shot ahead. She veered right and the car careened past on the left, on an angle, a sudden yank on the steering wheel. The brake lights dimmed and the vehicle sped into the distance. Tia hit the brakes, shoulder-checked: no more cars behind her. She let Pacifique catch up.

'I guess we're a bit invisible out here. I should get some lights,' Tia said.

'You couldn't be invisible if you tried,' chirped Pacifique. With her left hand she reached over and pinched Tia's haunch. She grinned when Tia shrieked, and the moment with the car was forgotten.

They found themselves at the water and took shelter against a tree cast on the sand years before. A gaggle of young men and women caroused around a campfire a hundred metres down the shore. Fog floated in. The carousers disappeared behind it, only the smell of smoke, the ringing of laughter and beer-bottle cheers giving them away, even the flicker of the fire muted. The fog wended through the roots and stumpy branches of their driftwood shelter. Within minutes, the moon veiled over and shrank into obscurity. The mist settled onto Tia's skin. She shivered. Pacifique shifted beside her and gathered her in her thin, warm arms. Tia let the heat from her lover replace the chill of the weather.

'Don't you feel like time accelerates when we're together?'

Pacifique's arms tightened around her.

'It feels like you just picked me up from school, but it must be pushing midnight now.'

'Time flies when you're having fun, isn't that what they say?'

'No. Not like that.' Annoyance slithered in between Tia's lips. 'It's like time operates differently with you and me.'

The fog and the ocean breathed around them.

'I feel it, too.' Pacifique's voice had grown sombre.

'Like we're in our own dimension, with our own rules.'

'I like that,' said Pacifique, the seriousness gone from her voice as quickly as it had appeared. 'A dimension all for us.'

Or like it's too good to be true, Tia thought. A spark somewhere deep inside her that wondered how real all of it was.

✳

She woke with a start. A man, unclear in the dark, stood above her.

'Hey, little lady.'

The sand beneath her an ice rink, the crick in her neck a vise.

'Somebody knows how to party,' said the man. Ashen dreadlocks draped his face, a giant nose with a mangled bridge. Broken a couple of times. He wore a Cowichan sweater. His breath bloomed in the cold.

Tia grasped the back of her neck with one hand and pushed herself to sitting with the other. She felt stiff with cold and confusion. A sea of beer bottles surrounded her. 'These aren't mine,' she said, her voice raspy. 'How long have I been asleep?'

'I've been tending the fire for the last hour. I just put it out and stumbled over you.'

Tia followed the man's gesture and saw the smoke drifting off a dying bonfire a few feet from them. Which she and Pacifique had seen from their perch some distance away. She turned and squinted into the dark. She couldn't make out their driftwood shelter. The fog had disappeared. Her body started to tingle, the blood coming back with pins and needles.

She struggled through the nauseating discomfort of limbs not quite attached, made for her feet.

'Let me help you,' said the man, taking her hand.

Tia yanked it away. 'No. That's fine. No. Thank you.' Something not right, something not okay. How had she come to be over here?

'Sorry.' A genuine softness in his voice, real contrition. 'I only – '

'I was with a friend.'

'Just you and me out here, I'm afraid. I'll walk with you. If that's okay.'

'No, my friend is here somewhere, I'm sure.'

'Everyone left.'

Then, a voice: 'Tiiiiaaa.' From over her shoulder.

Tia spun, searching for the source. Or from the waves? Soft, silky, and definitely Pacifique.

'Tiiiiaaa.' Louder. Behind her. Down the beach, from the driftwood shelter. Of course.

'Wait!' The man called as she ran, kept running, the driftwood pile farther away than she'd realized. The man's voice faded into the dark distance. Winded, she reached the shelter. Peered over the tree roots that rose out of the sand like a giant's hand, and found Pacifique sitting where she had left her, back against a log.

'You silly goose!' Pacifique said, and leaped to her feet. 'Running off on me.'

'You know I didn't,' said Tia. Frustration coursed through her veins. Pacifique must have known where she was. Why did she abandon her there to be woken by a strange man, in the cold, alone?

'Oh, dearest.' Pacifique shimmied over the log and came around the battered wood shelter. 'I'm sorry. I didn't mean it. I was just teasing.' She wrapped Tia in her arms and propped her head under Tia's chin.

The frustration slid from her skin. In its place, the same foreboding from that moment the other night when she had woken to find emptiness beside her in bed.

'It's okay,' Tia finally whispered, chin knocking against Pacifique's skull. 'Just don't do it again.'

*

'Things were going awry right from the beginning, then,' Andrew says later, in hospital.

'What do you mean?'

'You were in and out of it. Sometimes Pacifique was there, sometimes she was not.'

'She was there. I just ... thought she'd left.' A frail rebuttal. 'And anyway, that's not what the doctors say was happening. They have a different explanation.'

'Oh?'

'They say the whole thing was imagined after the fact. Trauma-induced psychosis. I wasn't sick before the bike accident.'

'Wait, they say you were sane, then you bonked your head and recreated a fantasy in the past?'

'Something like that.' Tia snorts.

'That, madam, is what I call a crazy theory.'

'Tell me about it,' Tia says, and laughs.

*

The sun rose on their backs as they pedalled from the beach to Tia's. They didn't speak. Tia's eyes burned. Sea air, too little sleep. She blinked hard, her lids tacky. Smooth black asphalt stretched ahead, clean in the new morning like it had been freshly laid. The paint dividing the road bright and mustard yellow. Tia edged her bike to the right and pulled into a driveway, took to the sidewalk. Trusted herself more there than on the road. The spaces between each square of concrete under her tires sounded a steady, rhythmic pulse, a heartbeat. Pacifique, on the road, tucked her tires close to the curb, pulled slightly ahead. The skin between the top of Pacifique's skin-tight black jeans and the bottom of her gold bomber jacket exposed to the cool winter air.

'Where do you go?' Tia whispered to the dawn.

'Hmm?' The sound carried over Pacifique's shoulder.

She couldn't have heard. 'Nothing. Just talking to myself.'

Pacifique slowed and they once again cycled abreast. 'What is it? What are you thinking?'

'Why ask? You always seem to know what I'm thinking.'

'I don't always know. Sometimes I'm guessing. It's not like you're difficult to read.'

Tia glanced at Pacifique, who wore not the familiar lopsided grin but a soft, kind smile. The faintest upturning at each corner of her mouth. Tia hadn't seen that look before, that sadness. What could Pacifique possibly be sad about? Tia took a deep breath and asked again, louder, 'Where do you go?'

Pacifique continued the lazy pedal along the curb, saying nothing.

'When you disappear, like last night?' Tia went on. 'For some reason I'm left alone at the bonfire, and that guy having no idea who you were. Or that night, at my house, when I woke up and you weren't in bed. Where do you go?'

Pacifique palmed her brakes and set one hot-pink Converse high-top on the damp curb. Tia halted with a jerk. Turned around on her seat to watch Pacifique hike the bubblegum-coloured cruiser onto the grass, set the kickstand. Tia swung a leg over her new ride, sparkling extra bright in the damp morning air, and leaned the bicycle against the arbutus tree in the nearest yard. Pacifique held out both hands, and Tia, not thinking of anyone or anything else, took them. Pacifique's hands burned, feverish and dry. A desert in this rainforest.

'I am always right here. Always. I need you to remember that.'

'Of course, but – '

'You're going to say you don't understand. Or, of course you'll remember this. I need you to promise me. This is important.'

Something like a tide pushed and pulled in her intestines. How long had she known this woman? Three days? Longer? A lifetime? The ebb or the flow, she wasn't sure, told her to listen.

'Promise me. Promise you will remember I am always right here. No matter what.'

'Oh, Pacifique, now you're scaring me.' The ebb and flow became a whirlpool, a riptide. 'This is weird. I didn't mean to offend you.'

She tried to pull away. Pacifique would not let go.

'Promise.'

'I promise.'

Pacifique waited, still clutching Tia's clammy hands.

'You're always right here. I'll remember, I promise. No matter what.'

Chapter 10

Riley does not hold Andrew's lapse against him, is used to it, knows, in part, what Andrew endures on a daily basis, the men having similar diagnoses. He makes no more attempts to flirt with Tia. In fact, later that evening, while Andrew lies sedated in his bed, running through the afternoon's events with the perspective provided by medication and the adrenaline crash, Riley confesses to Tia what it took him over a month to tell Andrew: he is not a doctor. Not a PhD candidate, or even master's-educated. In fact, he has completed only a couple of years of an undergraduate science degree. He says this to the floor, as he says most things, with a touch of contrition.

Andrew does not see this interaction. Instead he finds Riley pacing and muttering outside his door the next morning. A knife's tip of suspicion under Andrew's rib cage pulls away when Riley tells him he told Tia the truth.

As Andrew expected, Tia forgets his outburst in front of Riley and the three of them soon manage to spend time together as friends. Friends are the lights in a psych ward, and enemies the black holes ready to swallow any brightness, so it is best to keep even the assholes close, if you can. Riley could not be an asshole if he tried, Andrew reminds himself. Reminds himself that any man, even the kindest, humblest man, will puff up at attention from a pretty girl. Regardless, Riley has found his weak spot. No, not weak. Gaping, a wound. And Riley knows what he has found and understands why it is there. The bumbling bastard might be an awkward and friendless eccentric, but he is not stupid.

When he again sees Tia, who has grown accustomed to the sleep aids in her third week and rises in time to be in the common area before breakfast, she comes to him and lays her strong hand – he has imagined more than once those hands kneading the aches from his muscles, discovering the shape of him – on his arm, leaves it there, squeezes. It is as intimate as a hug in these parts.

A setback, that is all his explosion was. A setback in their future together.

*

Dr. Benson is not an attractive woman. She is not *unattractive* – rather, her appearance fails to register on Andrew. He does not consider her face, how its features fit, or the colouring of her cheeks, if she dyes her hair or whitens her teeth. He can say that she has plain brown eyes, a brown no one would ever call hazel, and he can say this because he finds it easy to look her in the eye. Even when things are difficult to talk about, as they are today, the day after his public temper tantrum.

Andrew is lucky this time around to have snagged the doctor under-stood to be, by most of the veterans, the best shrink around. For one, she is a woman, a rarity. This works in her favour: he cannot speak to what a female patient might think, but as a male patient who entered these walls covered in several layers of psychosis and machismo, he expected little. Turns out she knows his illness exceedingly well – and therefore, in part, knows him well – and won him over by the end of their first, and longest, session. He ceased to see her as a woman doing a man's job and simply as a doctor whose opinion he trusts. Briefly he wondered if she were operating outside the system, was a conscientious objector or maybe a mole. Then he dismissed this. After all, she medicates him, reprimands him for bad behaviour, and signs the papers that keep him hospitalized against his will.

Patients do not see their psychiatrists' offices. They are located else-where in the building or on the main hospital grounds across the road. This would necessitate a trip off-site, and although many of the patients are allowed out with doctor's permission, it is best to keep the inmates in. Therefore, Dr. Benson and Andrew meet in a corner at the junction where one patients' hallway meets the common area. The nurses' desk looms a few metres away.

Benson makes it simple. 'Be careful there.'

At first, Andrew does not follow. Only for a moment. 'Tia,' he says. 'Yes.'

Heat crawls like a rash up the sides of his neck and blooms across his cheekbones. He clenches his fists, fights the urge to bring a hand to his face. Instead, he smiles, a lopsided attempt at a grin.

Benson does not smile back. 'Your situation is not unique,' she says. 'This can be a place of high emotion. Research tells us that some of the strongest bonds are created in such situations. However, you're dealing with something else: mental illness. Tia is not well, not herself. Who you are getting to know in here may not be the person she really is.'

As if these thoughts have not already occurred to him, and numerous times.

'I know you know this,' Benson adds. 'I just wanted to remind you. You're on your way out of here. You don't need that kind of baggage.'

'Baggage!' Not a word he has heard her use.

'Look, Andrew, I'm not going to bullshit you.'

Another first: swearing. He feels a small twinge in his side.

'Tia is a beautiful girl. Bright. Pretty.'

How many pretty women had come across Benson's desk?

'She has suffered a serious breakdown. This is not the place to begin a romance. More than that, it is highly inappropriate.'

Any vestigial thoughts he has that Benson might be operating outside the system disappear. *Yes, ma'am*, let us uphold the system. At all costs. *Don't let the loonies fall in love.*

Don't let them even get close to something that might resemble love.

'Of course,' he says, back straight, accent smooth and light. 'Inappropriate. I get it.'

'You have to think of Tia, too. She doesn't need to deal with that right now. She needs to focus on getting well.'

Blah, blah, blah, he wants to say.

Instead he smiles blandly and stares at the skin between Benson's eyebrows, where a single near-black hair sprouts. It is not so much her tone, her admonishments, that bother him, it is something she said: 'You're on your way out.'

Days ago this would have been news worthy of a trumpet's triumph. Today it falls hard on his ears like a curse. An ugly deadline. He needs time.

✳

'She hasn't visited me,' is how it starts.

The three of them sit at a round table in the cafeteria, the kitchen closed until supper. The glaucous blue linoleum shines, still wet from the mop of the cleaner making his way through the unit. Bruce lumbers past, his skin shiny like the floor from what Andrew imagines is as many push-ups as he can manage with his softening physique. Bruce goes barefoot, leaves tracks. His face a blank slate. A setback. Andrew can see it in the slackness of the jaw, the distant stare. It happens. Rare to climb smoothly toward wellness here.

'Your mother?' asks Riley.

A silly question. Or a purposeful attempt to steer the conversation in another direction?

'Pacifique.' Tia says the name, not like a spell cast but like she might be talking about the weather, or a friend she knew in high school.

Andrew will not engage.

Riley will. 'Does she even know you're here?'

'She always knew things.'

'Like she was psychic or something?'

'Or something.'

Andrew says, 'What Tia is not telling you is that she did not see Pacifique for weeks before she got here.'

'Thank you, Andrew.'

It is the first time he has heard sarcasm from her.

'This is different. Now I'm here. I was sure she would come visit … '

'What Tia isn't telling you is that Pacifique is not real,' he blurts. His voice has risen a couple of notes and is touched with more emotion than he intends.

Riley shoots him daggers.

'That's what they say,' Tia says, her voice devoid of its usual defensiveness.

'What do *you* say?' Riley's tone is soft like a blanket. It is a real, human voice, untouched by the posturing he displayed during Tia's first weeks. Untouched by the tic, too.

'I say I don't see how she could be anything but real. I say how could someone *not* real make me feel so … '

Riley and Andrew do not need to share glances to know what the other is thinking. How can fantasy feel more like reality than anything they have ever known? How can fantasy make them feel more alive than anything real ever has?

'A doctor once said to me – this was years ago, when I was a teenager and the disease was, um, coming on, and, it was, what's it called, still unclear what it was – said to me, "If something seems too good to be true, it probably is." Like a telephone scam or a really good deal on a car, must be something wrong with it. Same with delusions. That's, um, what's it called, what this doctor said.'

'I think that's a stupid fucking thing to say,' says Tia, jaw tight. All calm replaced with the attitude Andrew has come to know. 'That's some stupid fucking doctor trying to shut you up, rope you in. That's a doctor who's never found true love.'

She stands and stalks across the common area, past the nurses' desk, so riled she cannot be bothered to care about how her behaviour might be read by her jailers. She disappears down the hall, toward her room, Andrew imagines, where she will sulk and talk to the wall. He has heard her – in those moments when he can steal a moment listening at her door – speaking to her imaginary lover. The perfect lover. It will take more than one lecture from a fellow psychotic to break this spell. Andrew is unperturbed. Although it is clear she will be certified for some time after he has been released, she has made it obvious that she understands the system. In another time, when his brain was locked into a different state, he would have taken her rant about 'fucking doctors,' about love, as a sign. Batty Andrew would have said this proved everything was moving along as planned, that all of this crazy was merely a bump on a road that promised so much more. He resists the temptation to turn her anger into something meaningful for both of them. Cannot banish the thought.

.

Chapter 11

They stole into the sleepy bungalow, giggled past Tia's roommates' closed doors, tripped over each other's feet, tumbled into bed. While the rest of the world roused itself and carried on doing all the regular things regular people do on a regular day, Tia roused something else, a part of herself that had lain dormant, the piece of her that lived to serve another woman. To serve Pacifique. And she was nervous. Not anxious, not buzzing with that constant readiness to fight or flee. No, these were the nerves of young love, of virginity leaving, the nerves of weak knees and flushed skin.

'You're shaking,' Pacifique said between kisses.

Tia sprawled on top of the smaller woman, leg draped over pelvis, propped on one elbow, hand free to stroke the black hair, the other hand tuning Pacifique's nipple. In lieu of responding, Tia dove in for another kiss, teeth grabbing the plum-coloured bottom lip that Pacifique offered. Ravenous.

She pulled back, sudden. 'I want to … I want … I don't know – '

Pacifique palmed the hair at the back of Tia's head and pulled, hard, until her own mouth touched the rings that looped through Tia's ear. 'Shh. Don't fret. Let go and everything will follow.'

A shudder like an earthquake cracked across Tia's vertebrae. A furnace blazed under her skin. Her breath came in rasps.

Pacifique released Tia's nape and guided her head until they were nose to nose. 'Kiss me. Slowly.'

Tia studied the eyes of the woman beneath her. In the bright yellow light of morning, they looked more brown than purple. The sadness that had flashed in them earlier was gone. They had become a pool, calm and clear, an invitation. *Jump in.* Tia brought her lips to the ones waiting, sweetly, light, eyes open. Kept them open, waiting to see the change in her lover's face. The pool shifted, the purple became dazzling, and the mouth opened wide like the tide going out, pulling Tia into a wild sea.

This time, Tia commanded the voyage. The blood-buzz smoothed into a lightly cresting wave and she rode it like she'd never been without sea legs. Rode it like the captain she could be with Pacifique. Pressed tongue into mouth, received the tongue offered in return. The wave that tumbled from Pacifique's mouth pushed her south, past the woman's small breasts, past the strange creature drawn with a dozen inked pins, past the whorl of belly button. She found the soft, dense bush, danced her fingertips through its curls, damper as she moved lower, until, with a gasp from her lover's mouth, she found what lay beneath. *Oh, what to do?* said a tiny voice. She silenced it with a deep breath and dove.

She knew this geography, but the path to Pacifique's orgasm would be unique. A new terrain, no map yet drawn. She tongued between the lips, dipped into the cavern, and then, nibble by nibble, found her way to the spot Pacifique had so deftly played on her own body. This time she would make Pacifique sing. The bundle of nerves an unfamiliar candy in her mouth, so different under tongue from her own clit under frantic fingers. With a lap across its head, it swelled, pushing past the shelter of the hood, and Pacifique jumped, a growl barrelling from her throat. Tia sucked, delicately, as if she were worried she might break it. Pacifique's thin fingers clutched her crown and pushed. Tia pulled deeper, created a vacuum in her mouth, and Pacifique shrieked. Tia popped up, but the woman under her would not – could not – meet her gaze, speak, assist, her body contorted into a C, bowing off the bed, her head cranked to one side, one hand balled into a fist against her forehead. With the other she tightened her grip on Tia's hair. *Keep going. By God,* the grip said, *keep going.* Tia flicked her tongue across the erect tip, and a shudder blasted through her lover. Pacifique's hand fell away. The legs on either side of Tia's head clamped around her skull. Tia flicked as fast as she could. She pulled away to lap and tongue and then dove back in. *Yes, yes, that.*

Chapter 12

Each morning, rise a bit earlier, or easier. Each day, be one morning closer to a morning outside *this fucking jail*.

Andrew waits for the moment his psychiatrist will decertify him. Knows it approaches. The patient must always be guessing. Give the patient his freedom long after he has earned it, or before he is ready. Never, ever give it to him when he expects it. They colour the release with benevolence, but it is yet another tragedy. *Go along, be free, you're well now*, they say. You are not well at all.

Each morning, he wakes closer to death. Death is the moment to rejoice, the true escape. It is birth that should be mourned. Andrew considers this as he shaves with the razor he has requested from the front desk. He no longer needs supervision – did he ever? A psych ward would be a terrible place to attempt suicide. And with a safety razor? Good luck. If he does not return within eight to ten minutes, a nurse will check on him. He is not permitted to close the bathroom door while he shaves. It does not matter: open or shut, the door has no lock. He draws the blade one final time across his jaw, less prominent under layers of fat put down with each antipsychotic swallowed. He studies the face reflected in the mirror. Is this what sanity looks like?

✳

They sit in the quartet of chairs near the nurses' station. The paranoia Tia carried when she arrived – the paranoia most patients bring in, like jackets pulled from the same closet – has eased, and it seems to him that she no longer believes the nurses can read her thoughts if she sits close to them. Andrew does not know if they even eavesdrop. Most of the time all they would hear are the ramblings of a crazy person, and the checkbox on their forms asks only one thing: *Crazy: Yes or No?* It does not matter to the nurses if one man claims to be Jesus of this neighbourhood and the next is Jesus of another. He senses that Tia has learned this, too, and with less of the psychotic high coursing through her system, she is quieter. In any case, the nurses work three metres away amid the clatter of chart clipboards on Formica counters, a television blaring for one of the Jesuses who sits with his nose inches from the screen, and the shriek of Mr. Park's runners as he and his Huntington's chorea dance up the hall: they cannot hear her.

After Tia tells him everything she is willing to, Andrew says, 'All of this over a woman you knew for five days?'

There must be more, a bedroom full of details.

'Oh, no, it was longer than that,' she says.

It is the end of Tia's third week in hospital, and the beginning of what looks to be his last.

'That is the whole story? The morning after the bonfire was the second-last day?'

'Yes. I remember that. I remember it all very clearly.'

'Then it was five days. That is only five days.'

Tia looks off to the side and sucks in a bit of her left cheek when she's thinking, her lips pursing as if she is going in for a kiss. She would probably think she looks silly – he has discovered as the high has worn off and the initial de-individualizing effects of the drugs have stabilized that she is highly self-conscious, as many anxiety-ridden people are – but he likes watching her in these moments. Likes the way the brain power required takes the edge off the rest of her, her body softer in the joints, the shadowed eyes briefly occupied with something else. She has those doe eyes that turn down at the outside corners. She always looks a little sad. He wonders, before he can stop the thought, if Pacifique liked that about her, that sweet, melancholy nature of her face, if she chose to fuck with her (or, hell, fuck her) because she thought she had found someone vulnerable enough.

Pacifique ain't real, you bugger, hisses a voice in his head. *If you don't get that through your thick fuckin' skull, you're not gonna be any help to your little friend.*

Andrew frowns. In the moments after the voice speaks, he cannot be sure it was not his own. People talk to themselves in their heads all the time, crazy or not. This fucking place. Second-guessing even the sane thoughts.

'What is your diagnosis?' Tia no longer stares into space; she stares at him. Did she catch him fighting with the forces in his head? Is that why she is breaking a cardinal rule of the place? He told her, in part, how he got here. He skipped daintily over the why. He thought, stupidly, that he had dodged a bullet.

'I have schizophrenia.'

Tia shrinks. He watches her unsuccessfully fight the reaction. The doe eyes register something akin to the fear he saw the day he lashed out at her and Riley.

'Oh,' is all she manages. She looks away, then back. Every movement measured. 'I'm sorry.'

'It's not a death sentence, Tia.'

'Of course not,' she says, too quickly.

'I had always been a strange kid. Lonely. "Doesn't play well with others" pretty common on report cards. That is partly why my parents sent me away. To Britain. For school. Thought I would do better in a stricter environment. The stress of moving back was too much. It was no longer my home.'

'Reverse culture shock,' she says.

'Exactly. And while I was better at keeping my temper, it was more like I was better at hiding things, hiding how I really felt. It snowballed, which is pretty classic. I started skipping class and did not even care to do my homework. Stayed in my room. Spent whole nights online. I started to invent new explanations for things. How the world should work. Try explaining to your own mother that you cannot possibly go to school because the teachers are agents of the government trained to brainwash you.' He laughs. An attempt at levity he does not feel.

'Crazy talk.'

'Precisely. I got kicked out of school. My mother said I could not live with them unless I got a job. I could barely get through a dishwashing shift without someone telling the manager I had said something weird. Done something weird. Started stealing, because I had been told to.'

'Money?'

'Dishware, utensils. They were symbols. I had to bring them home and catalogue them.'

'Holy shit,' says Tia.

Curiosity always the remedy to fear. And make it sound as if he no longer believes these things, that he, too, can hear how crazy it sounds.

'I got fired. Then I tried to burn our house down.'

'Oh my god, Andrew.' Tia grasps his forearm.

Arson doesn't usually bring out the sympathizers.

His stomach flutters. He stares at the hand on his arm. 'I was not much of a Boy Scout. Terrible at starting fires.' This time when he smiles, he means it.

Tia's grin lightens her face. The fear, the surprise gone. Two friends sharing war stories.

'And you wound up here, hey?' Tia says, shrugging. The points of her shoulders have softened in the past three weeks. She looks less underweight. The bingeing of the early days eased when lucidity returned. No more four-piece fish-and-chip lunches.

'Yeah. I had the brains – or lack of – to start the fire in my room while my parents were home. They smelled smoke and came running. I brandished a flaming cone of newsprint at my mother, told her not to get between me and my Capital M Mission. My father called the police. It did not take them long to realize I needed to be in hospital, not jail. My parents could have laid charges. It's a thing. Said to encourage accountability. They decided not to.'

Not that time, anyway.

(81)

'Imagine charging your own kid. You were sick, it wasn't your fault.'

'Yeah. Imagine.' He takes a breath. 'I was in hospital for a while that time. I had been sick for a long while, and it was a lot to get used to. This idea that my brain was – '

'Totally fucked,' Tia interjects.

Betrayal. That is what he had to get used to. His brain betrayed him.

She doesn't look at him when she says, 'I'm really sorry you had to go through that, Andrew.'

Normally he would say something polite. Proper. Normally he would play along. But today the perversity of it strikes him. He's the one who's fucking sorry. 'Yeah. Me too.'

She stares at the hands that clench and unclench in her lap. 'Do you think the same's gonna happen to me? Do you think they'll lock me up again? And again?'

'No.'

She swivels her head at his tone: so sure.

'No, I do not think so.'

He sometimes considers himself an expert. Most of the veterans do. Closing in on ten years of psychiatric care. Same amount of time spent living crazy as some of the new doctors have spent studying it. This is not about that. This is gut.

'I guess as long as I don't bonk my head again, I'm safe,' she says.

'Yes. Or at least wear a helmet next time.'

She grins. The bottom corner of one front tooth edges beyond the centre line, crowding its neighbour. In ten years, she will be covering her smile with a hand. He sees it, as clearly as he saw her future without another hospital visit. He pushes the vision further, trying to place himself beside her, ten years older, more definition in his cheekbones, acne scars finally faded. He cannot get there. She stands alone, unreachable. He shakes away the image. Shakes away the millisecond-long lightning strikes of white-hot pain that still come when he pushes his denatured brain.

She holds his eye and the grin slips away. She purses her lips and looks beyond him, over his shoulder. 'I gotta get out of this place.'

Chapter 13

Pacifique turned the clock on its head. She subscribed to no system of when to sleep and when to play. They had lain in each other's arms all day, and it was only once dusk fell that she left Tia's dishevelled bed. Pacifique slid off the mattress and dropped to the floor in a ball, hugged her knees, bounced up and down, as if preparing for takeoff, and then uncoiled in one sure, languid motion, her back to Tia. She raised her arms, a sun salutation, and rolled onto the balls of her feet. The calves in each leg popped. Ropes of hamstring became gluteals, which disappeared into erector spinae and obliques beneath her waist. Tia pushed herself up on her elbows and landed on the only interruption in the perfection of that back: the foreign, garish, and living ivory mask across Pacifique's left shoulder blade and up her neck. It couldn't be a birthmark. This was closer to a scar, an injury, the skin rough, damaged. Perhaps Pacifique wasn't untouchable after all. Pacifique dropped her arms and turned around.

'You're looking at my scleroderma again.' A twinge of an edge in her voice.

'I'm sorry. I shouldn't stare.' Where else to look? The only thing worth looking at was standing right in front of her.

'No. Look.' Pacifique dropped her bare bum next to Tia on the bed.

'Is it – ?' Tia started to ask and reached toward it, then stopped.

'Go ahead. Touch.'

Tia's hand hovered.

'It doesn't hurt,' Pacifique said.

Tia placed tentative fingers on the shield she had brushed so many times by accident. The skin was only rough where it joined the healthy skin it lay over. The whitish armour was smooth, slick, without texture. It felt like a reptile's hide.

'I'm shy about it.'

'I can't imagine you being shy about anything.' She squeezed the woman's leg.

'I'm like everybody else, Tia. Shy, vain.'

Tia sat up and took Pacifique's face in her hand. 'You're nothing like everybody else. You're magic.'

'It's you who is magic, Tia.'

Tia blushed. 'No. No, I'm average.'

The jaw in Tia's hand clenched. Pacifique grasped her wrist. 'Don't say that. Don't let anyone ever try to tell you that. You're not average, you're extraordinary. That's why I'm here, that's why I'm with you.'

✴

Andrew jumps on Pacifique's words.

'"That's why I'm here?" Oh, come on. That is messiah talk. Voices talk. Like she had been sent, or called upon. Crazy talk.'

'Something like that. I don't know, maybe she didn't say exactly that. It was a few months ago.'

Pacifique said exactly that. Time hasn't touched the memory. At the time it sounded weird. But now it sounds even weirder coming out of Andrew's mouth.

✴

Tia let the strange words float in the air and then let them go.

'Put on a dress,' Pacifique said suddenly. 'Something fancy. I'm taking you out. Gorgeous meal, wine.'

Tia didn't bother asking where, or protesting. She would have preferred to stay in bed for a few more hours, but maybe they needed a break. Some food. She couldn't remember the last time they had eaten.

She struggled out of bed, legs wobbly, knees achy from being bent at odd angles, kneeled upon. The carpet scratched the soles of her feet. She spread her toes, testing the fibres of the rug, how they pressed into the head of the first metatarsal bone, the edges of heels. The floor a part of a greater living thing, once a breathing, eating plant.

'Stop playing footsies with the carpet over there and find a dress,' Pacifique said from her vantage at the closet.

Tia laughed. 'I'm not sure I have one. A nice one, anyway.'

Pacifique, still naked, smooth and lithe in the falling night, reached into the closet and pulled out a hanger. 'What about this?' She held Tia's one and only little black dress. It was beautiful, but Tia hadn't worn it in years.

'Doesn't fit.'

Pacifique held out the hanger, grasped the hem of the garment and studied it. 'Try it.'

'It hasn't fit for years. Can't even get the zipper done up.'

Pacifique stared, unconvinced. 'You must have kept it for a reason.'

Tia took the dress, dropped the hanger, and stepped into the shift. She felt less resistance than she had expected as she pulled the sheer fabric over her hips. She shrugged one strap on, then the other, and felt for the zipper.

'Let me.' Pacifique sidled close to Tia's left hip, placed both hands on Tia's waist on either side of the open zipper, pressed heat through her palms, through the dress, into Tia's skin. Pulled her in for a kiss. A tongue darted across Tia's lips, and Pacifique zipped the dress. 'See, I told you,' she said, and stepped back.

Tia ran her hands over the front of the dress. It was snug, but it fit. 'You're a miracle worker. I kept this thing 'cause I like it so much. I didn't think I'd ever get into it again.'

'It's because you haven't been eating enough. That's my fault. By the end of tonight, you'll be busting out of the thing. That's my plan.' Pacifique spidered two fingers across Tia's silky stomach and pinched her soft belly.

'You devil,' Tia said, lunging.

Pacifique leaped out of reach, a grin splashed across her face.

Softer, Tia said, 'Come here.'

Pacifique dropped to earth, returned to Tia's side, wrapped her arms around the taller woman's waist, and looked into her face.

'I love you,' Tia said.

The violet eyes swam in a shallow sea.

Tia bent to Pacifique's soft cheek, cupped one tear with her mouth, licked. Caught the other tear with a finger she grazed along Pacifique's jawbone. 'So much. For always.'

'Promise?' Pacifique asked.

'I promise.'

Tia would realize later that she didn't know what the promise would require. Didn't know she couldn't possibly promise such a huge, heavy thing. Love forever, unless … *Unless you go away, sweet Pacifique,* she should have said. *Unless you leave me. If you go, I will have to reconsider.*

Pacifique broke the moment with her signature grin, white teeth flashing. 'Now we find me a dress,' she announced.

'Oh? Can't you wear – ?' Tia looked around the room. 'What you were wearing earlier?'

'And where, dear Tia, might I find what I was wearing earlier?'

Tia lifted an item from the nearest pile, only to find a ball of unidentifiable fabric underneath – a sheet, her clothes, Pacifique's? 'Okay, well. I don't know where your clothes are.'

'I'm not sure they're here anymore. Was I even wearing clothes? I seem to remember a lot of nudity.'

'I concur. We have been naked forever. There were never any clothes.'

'Sounds like heaven to me,' said Pacifique, stepping over the textile mountain at Tia's feet. 'You, naked, most of the time. And, once in a while, you in that dress.'

'Stop that talking or we'll never leave this bedroom.'

'And there would be nothing wrong with that. But you're right. I want to take you out. And I still need a dress.' Pacifique returned to her perch in front of the closet.

'I don't know why you're looking in there. Everything I have is going to be way too big for you.'

'Hmm, what about this?' asked Pacifique, pulling out a lime-green outfit Tia didn't recognize. 'It matches your new bike.'

'What is that?' She held out a hand.

Pacifique ignored it. 'This will work.'

'I don't remember having that. Whatever that is.'

'I think it's a dress. A skirt? Do you have a safety pin?'

'Somewhere. Not in here. I'll go look.' Tia pulled on the bedroom door, sticky in the frame gone wonky with the shifting of the house, with the moisture in the air, and stepped into the hall. She couldn't remember the last time she'd seen her roommates. She supposed at class the other day she saw Melissa. Esther, however, she couldn't say. The house felt vacant. Cold. Stale. Goosebumps scattered up one side of her neck and down the other. She shook them off with a brisk wiggle of her shoulders and started going through drawers in the living room. Esther sewed, left bits and bobs everywhere, had made their curtains, once hemmed a pair of Tia's pants. And, yes, had abandoned a handful of safety pins in a drawer.

In the bedroom, a woman in green spun in circles, one hand clutching fabric to her hip. The dress – for it was now somehow a dress, draped over one shoulder, leaving the other bare, and billowing out at her feet like a sail – shimmered, caught what light was left in the sky outside Tia's bedroom window. Pacifique's skin glowed.

'You're a dream. How did you do that? I'm sure that's not my dress.'

'I don't think it was a dress. I'm not even sure it's a skirt. Pin?' She took the safety pin, hooked it through the layers bunched at her hip, then released both hands. 'Ta-dah!'

'Is there anything you can't do?' Tia shook her head.

'I'm sure there's something. Now, put these on and let's go.' She gestured to the shoes she'd set by the door, a pair of sky-high heels Tia remembered buying on a whim years ago for a cousin's wedding, casting them aside at the last minute because she realized she couldn't stand in them. 'I couldn't find anything for myself, Ms. Bigfoot.'

Tia slid her size nine foot into one shoe, leaned down to help ease her heel in, and tentatively straightened the leg. Not bad. Pacifique held out a small hand and Tia grabbed it, stepping into the second shoe. 'Forget about Bigfoot. I'm going to be Godzilla in these next to you.'

'Shh, come. I was only teasing. I'll help you.'

They left the bedroom, Pacifique going ahead, Tia using the wall for support. Each heel sounded like a heartbeat on the hardwood floor. She couldn't remember feeling so powerful in the shoes before, so sexy. She pictured herself as a long, lean line. She stopped and looked over her shoulder, studied how the calf curved into ankle, ankle into three inches of thin heel. 'Yes. Yes, I like this.'

'Who are you talking to?' Melissa, in her room. Tia hadn't noticed the door ajar, the room occupied. The bedside lamp cast a feeble glow in the corner of Melissa's bedroom. Melissa sat as close as possible to the light, a book splayed on her knees. She wore a sweatshirt, its cuffs rolled, sweatpants, thick wool socks.

'Oh! I didn't know you were home. I'm going out. See you tomorrow at school.' Tia tiptoed away, trying not to clack against the floor.

Behind her, Melissa called out: 'Tomorrow's Sunday, Tia! No school.' And then, something else, faint, something that sounded like, 'Not that it matters to you.'

'Hurry! I'm hungry,' Pacifique said from the door. She stood in the green dress and her black Converse sneakers. 'Think it works?' she asked, and curtsied.

'Hell, yes. You'd rock that outfit in snowshoes.'

Pacifique laughed, a sound like raindrops hitting windows. 'I like the way you think.'

Tia grabbed a coat and they were off into the night.

✳

'Where did you go?' the shrink asks her. 'For dinner.'

The man takes a different tack every day. Sometimes he asks her to deconstruct each moment, find all the holes, lay it open for the fallacy it is. Sometimes he pretends he believes.

'Brava.'

'The Italian place on Wharf Street?'

'Yes.' One beat, and then two. She has managed to surprise the doctor. 'A real place. No mysterious disappearing nightclub or generic coffee shop.'

'I hear that sarcasm. I'm curious: Why do you think that is? Why do you think for your last night Pacifique took you to a place you could go back to? You did go back, right?'

'Yes. Of course.'

'And had anyone seen her? Did they remember the two of you being there?'

He knows she went from one place to another for a month and all she heard was, 'No, sorry.'

'Tia?'

'I heard you.' Tia petulant like a teenager, voice loud with anger. 'No. Okay? Nobody saw her. Nobody remembered her.'

'Don't you think it's curious she took you to a real place?'

'It was a good restaurant. Pacifique wanted to take me somewhere nice.'

'Tia, Pacifique isn't real. The two of you never went to that restaurant. My question is why your delusion took you in that direction, instead of taking you to another mystery location, like the nightclub. I feel like that was a breakthrough. I think it's possible your brain was creating … landmarks.'

We went there, we went there, we went there.

'Or, say, markers. Checkpoints. Was this real, yes or no? The real setting allowed you to go back later and see that the event never happened.'

I know we went there.

'Unfortunately, it didn't really work. Which is part of the reason you're here.'

They ate insalata caprese and linguine aglio e olio and roasted eggplant and three desserts because Pacifique couldn't decide, and by the end of the evening the little black dress felt very little indeed, as Pacifique had said it would, and when they left the restaurant Tia let out the zipper and hugged her coat closer, and something about having a couple of drinks on board made walking in the heels easier.

She wants to say all of this. Instead, she says, 'Have you ever had roasted eggplant, Dr. O'Shea?'

'Excuse me?'

'Have you ever tried roasted eggplant?' She repeats it slowly.

'Sure. Of course.'

'Roasted. Grilled.'

'Oh, yes. I went to Tel Aviv once. Stayed at the Ritz Carlton in Herzliya.' He grins, a man in a credit card commercial. 'Every morning there was the most incredible spread: hummus and fresh bread and olive oil and, yes, roasted eggplant. I haven't thought about that for some time.'

'It was delicious.'

'You bet.'

'Say you went back to Israel, went back to the Ritz Carlton, and at breakfast you didn't find eggplant. When you asked, they said they didn't have it. They told you that they had never served it. Who would you believe? Some hotel employee? Or your memory?'

'Tia. Eggplant is different from a person.'

'That's not the point. I'm asking, who would you believe?'

'Well, I suppose I'd evaluate the evidence. Do my research. If it turned out I was wrong, then so be it.'

'Oh, fuck you.'

The doctor stares, his typical non-response.

'You'd believe your own fucking memory and you know it. Now imagine that eggplant wasn't the most amazing eggplant you'd ever eaten but the most amazing person you'd ever known. Wouldn't it break your heart to hear time after time that no one believed? No one.'

'Tia, I know this is hard for you, but – '

'That's the problem, doc. You don't know a goddamned thing.'

Chapter 14

Tia picks at the peeling wooden arm of the chair. It is Mr. Park's chair, his name written in Sharpie on a piece of printer paper taped to the back. Mr. Park has not been around for a couple of days. Bruce says he died. More likely they moved him to the seventh floor.

'They say I am sane,' Andrew says.

'Bullshit. Prove it.'

'I don't have to,' he says. 'It is written right there in my chart. Doctor's orders.'

'Not sure it means much if these people say you're not crazy.'

Andrew follows her wave to the nurses' station. He laughs. She allows a smile.

'What about you?' he asks.

'What do you mean?'

'When are you outta this joint?'

She stifles a chuckle. Tia, she is allowed to laugh at him. A little.

She sighs, exhaling through puffed cheeks. 'Pacifique hasn't come. I haven't seen her … I can't remember. It's been a long time.'

Only a week ago, Tia would have tried to count how many days it had been.

'She is likely not coming.' He means no unkindness. He is merely reading the data.

'Probably not.'

Andrew blinks through his squint, masking it.

'No, that's not right,' she says. 'She's not coming. She's not. If she was going to come, she'd have come already.'

'I think you are right,' Andrew says, and hears a touch of the patronizing tone he sometimes takes. 'So?'

'Haven't figured that part out yet, Andrew,' she replies, the edge creeping in.

It happens less, this irritation, but it continues to come. Her brain has a limit, still. 'I'm sorry.' She is allowed to laugh at him. He, in turn, will give her what he rarely gives anyone else: sympathy.

Tia shoots him a suspicious look.

He bows his head, stares at the hands in his lap.

'It's fine,' she says. 'Don't worry about it.'

'I am supposed to have my stuff cleared out by eleven. They need the bed. I should go.' He stands. Does not leave. Cannot. 'Um … I – '

'Yes, Riley?'

He laughs a proper laugh. Tension leaks from his knees. Tia smiles at him from her perch on the chair. They have come to be regulars at the visiting area kitty-corner from the nurses' desk. Nobody visits, so the chairs are usually free. Even Mr. Park, when he is around, spends more time pacing the halls than using his chair. Tia wraps her arms around one leg. She's got her own T-shirt on but hasn't changed out of the baby-blue flannel pants. He remembers the way the hospital pyjamas, washed a hundred – a thousand – times felt against his skin, wonders how much softer the skin on the inside of Tia's wrist would be.

'What?' she prompts.

Andrew takes a deep breath, blows it out through pursed lips. 'I just – I do not want to say goodbye.'

'Oh. Okay. That's fine. You don't have to.'

'No, that is not what I mean. I mean … What if I did not say goodbye because this was not going to be the last time I saw you?'

'You mean you want to visit?'

'Sort of.' It is not what he means.

'Tell me.'

'I am not sure I can visit. You know? Once you are out of this place, it is not a place you want to come back to.'

She lets him worry his way through this.

'What if I visited you after? After you are out?'

The surprise on her face is matched only by his hurt. They have spent almost every day together these past four weeks. That is months in outside-time. That must mean something to her.

Not the first time you've had a girl on the inside, boy.

Andrew grits his teeth. *This is different.*

'Sure,' she says. 'Why not?'

It is not what he had hoped but better than he expected. He finally meets her gaze.

'Get packed, Andrew. You don't want them changing their minds.'

Whatever that moment was, it is gone. Andrew turns and walks away. He does not look back as he returns to his room. Not his room anymore, just a place he slept for months, where he went from crazy to sane.

Chapter 15

Before he is released, Andrew stops asking Tia for the story of the accident. Did he simply lose interest, she wonders. Or did he give up? Maybe he got a lecture from the lady doctor about feeding Tia's delusions. Or maybe he realized she honestly couldn't tell him what he wanted to know. The accident itself remains invisible to her. An entire corner of the puzzle is missing. The harder she pushes, the more it fades. This memory loss feels like a shard of truth. O'Shea says it only proves his point, but she thinks it makes sense she has forgotten. How is she supposed to remember what happened before she cracked her skull against the asphalt?

She remembers they went back to her house after dinner. It was pushing midnight by then. They didn't have sex. They dropped their evening wear on the floor, gathered the blankets and sheets, crawled underneath, and fell asleep in each other's arms. She remembers they woke with the dawn and dressed without speaking. Pacifique found her street clothes from the day before somewhere under the bed. Creases stretched diagonally across the chest of her torn T-shirt. Even dressed like a vagrant, she dazzled. Frost coated the bedroom window. Tia pulled on another layer.

It was cold. Like the night they had met. The snow, however, had melted. Instead, hours-old rain glistened on the streets. The sky beamed a clear, open blue. Pacifique took off one pair of mini-mitts and gave them to Tia. They collected their bikes from the shed, pushed them to the front lawn, stood on the crisp grass. Pacifique was unusually quiet. Mouth set, no smile. For the first time, she looked tired.

✳

'How old was she?' O'Shea asks.

'Young. Younger than me. Or my age,' Tia replies.

Hard to say.

✳

That morning, their last morning, Pacifique looked like someone who had seen a lot of life, more life than a twentysomething would have seen. Burdened.

'You pick,' Pacifique said after several moments of silence.

Why did she ask that of her? Is it Tia's fault they found themselves in the town across the bridge, on unfamiliar streets, steep and slick? Is it Tia's fault she pulled ahead, so that when –

The memories stutter to a stop. She can't be sure she was in front when the accident happened. She has never been able to recall the actual crash. That's the only certainty she has. The certainty of a blank space, a black hole in her recollection. No way to know how much time passed between hearing Pacifique's laughter behind her and the accident.

The memory gives her nothing. Answers nothing. There is no truth there.

Chapter 16

Rachael, the new girl, takes the pack of Belmonts proffered by the nurse Big Bernadette. 'Where did you look?' Rachael asks Tia.

'Everywhere,' says Tia. She follows Rachael to the sign-out book, which lies open on a small table underneath the clock next to the nurses' station. 'Everywhere we'd ever been. Everywhere I thought she might go.' Under 'Reason,' Tia writes what Rachael wrote: 'smoke.' They have ten minutes.

Rachael arrived at Ian Charles the day after Andrew left. If Tia hadn't watched her being admitted, she might have wondered if she was a new patient at all. She has no anxious energy about her, no story about how there was once a nationwide warrant out for her arrest, or how she was responsible for saving Canada Post millions of dollars because she invented new 'pallet technology,' as Jake once claimed he had.

Tia punches the Down button for the elevator. Fights against the urge to glance back. She's allowed to do this, after all. She's not even leaving the building.

Rachael is model-beautiful. Big, juicy lips, wide-set eyes, arching brows freshly waxed. Like she went to the salon on her way to the psych ward. Rachael is voluptuous on the bottom – big ass, meaty thighs – and narrow up top. She wears a close-fitting, V-neck T-shirt, and through it Tia sees the ridges of a padded bra. They step into the elevator and Rachael leans forward to press '2.' The cups of her bra gape.

'What about her apartment?' she asks. 'She wasn't there?'

'I couldn't find it,' Tia says. 'I walked around that neighbourhood for hours, day after day. I could never find her street. I found some houses that looked similar, houses built around the same time, even some with the same bay window. They didn't have the right stairs, or any stairs at all. A couple of times I got so desperate I went to the top floor, even knocked once.'

That time, she found someone home. The man who answered – handsome, grizzled from a couple of days without shaving, tattoos peeking out beneath the cuffs of his long-sleeved shirt – looked almost familiar. By then, everyone looked both familiar and absurd. Her mother, worried because she hadn't heard from Tia since driving her home from the hospital, Tia in a sling, had asked – instructed – her to come over. Tia had managed an hour-long visit, and by the end of it she wasn't sure her mother was her mother, her face a mismatched mosaic of pieces from other people's faces, the once-familiar nose and circles under the eyes that Tia had inherited now foreign, a mask.

The elevator opens onto the darkened second floor. On Saturdays, nothing happens here. No outpatient group therapy, no art class. For a moment, Tia feels alone, the first breath of solitude she's had since she landed in this place.

'Look, you might get in trouble,' she says to Rachael. 'Asking me about Pacifique? It's not really encouraged. Talking about her like she's real.' The dim hallway stretches ahead of them, closed office doors on either side like sentries marking their passage.

Rachael pauses and bends to scratch behind her knee. Leggings stretch over her butt and legs and her shirt inches up, revealing a smooth lumbar spine. Muscles ripple under the fabric. For some reason, Rachael isn't wearing hospital pyjamas. *Lucky.* Tia has been allowed, finally, to wear her own clothes during the day. Her mother didn't bring pyjamas, though, so every night Tia puts on the flannel uniform. At least she doesn't have to don the royal-blue and caution-yellow duds the high-flight-risk patients must wear, and not just to bed. One afternoon she watched from her window while Caveman sped across the street to the coffee shop. He was brought back to the ward a few minutes later in the company of two guards. He was smiling, a giant paper cup of sugary caffeine clenched in one rough fist.

'I've gotten over my "diagnosis phase,"' says Rachael, straightening, 'but really, I don't put much stock in the theories these people pass off as "truth." It's not truth, it's guesswork.'

They approach an unlit room at the end of the hall.

'My guess is that you actually should talk about Pacifique, because you need to understand. Understand what happened. It's like working through a problem. Try telling someone who's lost someone to cancer or, like, gotten their heart broken that they can't talk about it. It's bullshit. I won't bother you to talk about her any more than you want to. But I'm curious. I'm always curious why people are here, and who they've loved.' Rachael talks like a news anchor, fast and precise and like she has a point to make in a limited amount of time.

'Imagined,' Tia corrects. 'Who they've imagined.'

They step into the music room, so-called because an out-of-tune piano occupies a dank corner. They're not here for music, they're here for the roof garden, which they access through a door on the opposite wall.

'I tend to use both terms loosely.' Rachael laughs, a wide, raucous laugh that would sound perfect echoing off the smoky walls of a beer-soaked pub. Not the kind of laugh for this place. 'Shit, the number of boyfriends who've called me a crazy bitch on their way out the door? Imagined. Loved. It all boils down to the same thing.'

'Can't say I know what you mean.'

'Basically, I'm saying it doesn't hurt to believe in Pacifique.' Rachael pushes the emergency-exit door, which promises to signal an alarm and does no such thing. A seaweed-scented gust hits their faces. 'Imagined or real, she was a part of you. *Is* a part of you. How is Pacifique different from me being in love with a man who barely knows I exist?'

The door slams behind them, and Tia jumps, resisting the urge to lunge and snag the door handle. Would it be so bad if they got locked out? Locked out of jail?

'Sure, he has a driver's licence and a house I can actually locate, but what we have is all in my head. Same thing. Same outcome. Just like I have to get over him, you have to get over Pacifique. And you do that by forgetting. It's not about finding peace with it, because there's no peace. There's no closure. You just forget. Block it out. Strike the record from your brain.'

'Nobody's suggested anything like that before.'

Rachael offers Tia a cigarette. Muscle memory kicks in as she cups her hands around the flame. Against what wind, she wonders, and scans the imposing walls that surround them on four sides. She exhales, imagines two of her stacked head to toe. Their enclosure must rise twelve feet in the air at least. At the top, barbed wire in lazy, unkempt loops.

Rachael triple-puffs on her cigarette. Smoke leaves her nose as fresh smoke enters her mouth. She exhales long and slow, looks over Tia's left shoulder, shakes her head. 'You have no idea how many fucked-up things I've had to forget and move on from. Like the time I used my mother's credit card to buy a plane ticket to Scotland to meet some guy I'd chatted with online for a few hours? Stole a bunch of cash from her, too, got to ye olde Caledonia, never found the guy, got fucked up on booze and drugs, and wound up in a place like this. There's no coming to terms with something like that. I'm kind of a pro at putting things behind me.'

'Maybe you can help me.' The words escape from Tia's mouth. That isn't what she meant to say, is it? She leans on the lip of an empty planter box. It's called the roof garden, but the institution hasn't bothered to plant anything. Concrete underfoot, concrete walls, dead garden plots, and a hoop sans net. A deflated basketball languishes in a puddle near the northwest corner.

'Maybe,' answers Rachael. 'Everything happens for a reason, that's what I say. Isn't it great I came right when you were ready to get better?'

'Ready? You think I'm ready?' Dampness from the garden box seeps through Tia's jeans. She returns to her feet, puts the cigarette to her mouth. Nicotine buzzes in her fingertips and leaves cotton balls in her brain.

'Yeah. I see it. You're tired of this place. And you're tired of being broken-hearted. There's a point in every relationship where you realize enough is enough. You hope there is. Not everyone has that wisdom. That strength. To leave.'

'This whole time they've been telling me it wasn't a relationship, that I was ill, to treat it like fantasy.'

'Whatever floats your boat, chica. I see you here, in a fucking mental hospital, still choked over some bitch who dumped your ass without the courtesy of a goodbye and I think whatever they've got you doing to, you know, cure yourself, it ain't working.'

Softly, angrily: 'She's not a bitch.'

'I believe you. I believe she's not. But what she did was a bitchy move. Like undeniably bitchy. Cold. Heartless. You can't deny that.' Rachael gestures with the cigarette, an exclamation mark in space.

'I don't know the whole story. It's hard to say for sure she up and left. Maybe she was taken away, or ...'

'Or?'

'Or ... or something! I don't know. I just know she's not a bitch.' Tia takes a long drag, swallowing the cough that crawls up her windpipe.

'She didn't get taken away. What, in the minutes between you bonking your head and waking up, she got, like, abducted by aliens? She's getting anally probed right now instead of being your girlfriend?'

Tia snorts.

'Good. You still have a sense of humour.'

'Of course not. Of course she didn't get abducted.'

'And there's the whole issue of the woman who saw you, who called for help, who didn't see anyone with you.'

'Yes, yes, but that's just what I remember. That day is gappy. Huge blocks of time I can't account for. I have a feeling there was something between my last memory and the accident. What about the time I was unconscious? Or too out of it to properly create any memories? I could have lost an entire half-hour.'

'Okay, say you forgot about the last, what, ten minutes before the actual accident? What's the likelihood that Pacifique was more than a block behind or in front of you?'

'It's possible.'

'How likely?'

'Pacifique had disappeared on me before.'

'You did notice when you were telling me about that that she only ever disappeared when you'd been sleeping? You would wake up and she wouldn't be there.'

'It's still possible.'

'Sure, maybe. Unlikely, though, given her history. More importantly, running off and leaving you high and dry is a super bitchy move. You've told me she's not a bitch. It would be totally out of character, therefore, for her to ditch you like that, for months on end. So she didn't go anywhere.'

'So … wait. What? So you're saying she didn't leave? She was there?'

'No. I'm actually saying the opposite, Tia.'

Rachael sighs, drops her smoke to the damp concrete and takes Tia's free hand. Tia fights against the urge to pull away, leaves her hand limp in the other woman's strong warm ones.

'She didn't run away,' Rachael says. 'She didn't get abducted. She wasn't seen by the woman who called 911. Or anyone else, for that matter. And you can't remember what happened before the accident.'

'Yeah, I hit my goddamned head, Rachael.' She yanks her hand back. Puts the end of one thumb into her mouth, begins to chew, then remembers the cigarette. It tastes like soot.

'Pretty hard. You were in hospital for a couple of days, right? That's more than a bonk on the head. That's a brain injury.'

'Yeah, I'm not an idiot. I had bleeding on the brain, a serious concussion, blah blah blah.'

'Pacifique wasn't there,' Rachael cuts in.

'I know, I know. I imagined her.'

'I'm not saying that.'

'What?' Tia flicks the cigarette, and it spins end over end before landing in the next garden box. She takes one step back.

'Wait. I sort of am. But not exactly.'

'Oh my god, you're fucking mental.' Tia turns a shoulder to Rachael. Her pants cling, wet, to her buttocks. It can't be more than ten degrees on the roof garden.

'So I hear. I'm saying – for Christ's sake, Tia, look at me – I'm saying she wasn't there. That the accident did not happen the way you partially remember it. That you were alone when you flew off that bicycle. Because no other explanation makes sense.'

Tia doesn't answer and Rachael doesn't push. Eventually, she points her chin at the door and Tia nods. She holds the door, and Tia passes through into the warmth of the quiet music room. They traverse the empty hallway, wait in silence for the elevator, and rise without saying a word.

'If I imagined that, what else did I imagine?' Tia says in the moment before the elevator door opens, voice low, a whisper.

The door slides open and spits them onto the fourth floor. They take turns at the sign-out book. Their return has caught the attention of a trio of patients watching *Poltergeist* on the TV in the other corner of the ward. One man lies on his stomach, chin in his hands, feet waggling in the air. Another lies stretched across the entirety of the peach-coloured couch. The third, a woman, sits curled in on herself on the ratty rocker next to the sofa.

'That's the big question, isn't it?' Rachael says as she signs her name.

Without speaking, they settle in the visiting area.

It's Tia who breaks the silence. 'It's a choice, then.'

'Yup. Breaking it into logical pieces will only take you so far. God's existence cannot be deduced by reason alone.'

'Huh?'

'Faith. It's faith. For a lot of people, their faith allows them to believe in a fantasy. I think God is a crock of shit, but I get the attraction. God is a highly attractive force. You believe in Pacifique. You have the faith that everyone else lacks. Problem is, you tell people you believe in God, they don't lock you up. Your faith in that fantasy doesn't harm you; in fact, it's pretty much universally accepted. You believing in Pacifique is heresy. Sick. So you make a choice. Continue having faith, because logically you can't prove your fantasy is real. Or give in to the supposed logic professed by everyone else and deny that belief. When I said Pacifique wasn't there when you had your accident, I meant it. In a way. As far as the rest of the world is concerned, Pacifique wasn't there. You want to live in this world, you gotta toe the line.'

'It's unfair.'

'It is. But what's your alternative?'

'Rotting away in this shithole.'

'Yup. Or dividing your allegiances. Believing inside that Pacifique is real and pretending for everyone else's benefit that she's not. Why make it difficult for yourself? Drink the Kool-Aid, take the blue pill.'

'Are you Pacifique?' Riley's voice a snake's hiss behind Tia's head.

She jerks around, finds the short man staring over her shoulder at Rachael. 'Jesus, Riley. You scared me.'

'Yeah, dude. What the fuck?'

Tia doesn't know how Rachael can make the hardest sounds in the English language sound like oil dripping from a bottle.

'We're not all the same, Riley. Get your minorities straight, hey?' Rachael's voice rises at the end of every word for a moment, Valley girl–style.

'Of course. Of course. Of course.' He says the words like a hymn. 'I'm sorry.' He steals down the hall and disappears into a room. Not his room, Tia notes, and shakes her head.

'Wow, he's worse,' Tia says.

'Yeah, he's in and out of here more than a bulimic in a bathroom. I'm not sure he's ever gonna get any better.'

'Oh, you know him?'

'Hell, yeah. I met Dr. Riley years ago. We seem to have similar schedules for some reason. But he's never here voluntarily.'

'That goes without saying.'

'I'm here voluntarily.'

'Oh.' Tia doesn't know what that means. Surely no one would *choose* to be here.

'I get sick. I go off my meds, don't get back on them soon enough, or the meds stop working, or never really worked in the first place. I start fucking nasty-ass dudes from the bar and maxing my credit card and, like, understanding the universe and shit?' Her voice goes Valley girl again and she hangs her mouth open, the jaw slack. Tia laughs. 'When God starts talking to me, I know I'm seriously fucked. There's always a part of me, sometimes a minuscule part, that knows I'm crazy. And tells me so.'

'That's a trip.'

'Yeah, that whole, "If you think you're crazy, you're not" line is bullshit. If you think you're crazy, you should look into it.'

'Everyone comes in here claiming that they're sane.'

'That happens to me, too. I'm not always on top of my brain. I have good friends, though. Friends who know what's up with me, who tell me when I'm acting like a fucking freak.'

'Your friends … know?'

'Oh, yeah. Good luck hiding being a nutbar from your friends. Might as well be straight about it.'

'Andrew knows I'm crazy.'

'He your friend?'

'Sort of,' Tia answers. Is he? 'He was a patient, a veteran. Maybe you know him. Andrew Purser? Schizophrenic?'

'Don't think so.'

'He's not much taller than me, brown hair, kinda pudgy. Except I think that's the drugs. He's really sweet.' He is, Tia realizes. She hasn't described a man as 'sweet' in a long time.

'Nope, definitely not. The only Andrew I knew was borderline and about five feet tall.'

'Borderline what?'

'Borderline. Borderline personality disorder. Not much for someone like that in the loony bin. Gave him a whole cocktail of drugs and all that happened was that when he left, he was addicted to lorazepam.'

'Oh.' Tia takes lorazepam almost every day. Less recently, but it's part of the routine. The stuff works as well here as it did on the outside. Like marijuana without any side effects. Except, of course, for the addiction. 'Andrew helped me a lot in here.'

'Good. Of all places, here is where you want someone like that.' Rachael sighs. Her ebullience comes in fits, and she doesn't have much left. They've been talking too long. Rachael captures time, captures your imagination, makes you forget you're not here by choice. Like Pacifique.

'Who helped you, your first time here?' Tia asks. A shadow drops over Rachael's face. It is perhaps the most personal question Tia has asked since Rachael arrived.

'Nobody. I was batshit and a Black woman. Nobody gave a fuck about me. I fought like a cat in a bathtub to get out of here. I escaped. Twice. Second time, I was brought back in handcuffs and sent to lockdown. Didn't see a human who wasn't staff or a patient for three weeks. They beat you down that way. I didn't have anyone.' Rachael huffs, a sound somewhere between a chuckle and what comes out when you're punched in the gut. 'Even Dante had Virgil to guide him through hell. But then Dante was white, wasn't he?'

Rachael stands, fixes her T-shirt, and clears something that could be tears from her throat. Her face remains impassive. She doesn't look at Tia when she says, 'See ya later, okay?'

Without waiting for a response, she's off down the hall, into a room, and the door shuts with what is as close to a slam as you can get here, a firm whoosh of air pushed out, a small piece of control exerted, the patient closing herself in her cell.

✳

Rachael doesn't stay long. One day, she's babbling next to Tia at breakfast, the next she's not. Simple as that. O'Shea says Rachael was discharged. 'She just got here!' Less than a week and already released?

'She's done her time,' he says, ignorant of the incarceration storyline he has walked into. 'Subsequent hospitalizations tend to be shorter.'

Tia had tried to figure out how many times Rachael had been admitted, without asking outright, and came out with a number verging on half a dozen. She was nothing like Riley, spewing conspiracy theories, or Bruce and his quiet, constant drawing, the out-of-nowhere pronouncements of love for his 'fiancée,' a woman it was said had taken a restraining order out on him. Nothing like Caveman, with his predilection for hyper-sweet espresso drinks, years of street life and drug use written like a map across his face. Or even like Andrew, who up until Rachael's arrival had been Tia's benchmark for 'sanity.' Rachael had a vitality most people lacked, a vivacity that would get her called eccentric by some. Tia knows why she has so many boyfriend – and ex-boyfriend – stories: she is magnetic. She takes nobody's shit.

Now she's gone. Tia doesn't know her last name, what neighbourhood she lives in, what she does for a living. If she has a living. She could be like Bruce or Andrew, both of whom have wealthy parents who've orchestrated some kind of allowance for their sick sons. She could be on disability. One woman told Tia about her gorgeous condo apartment downtown, paid for in part by a cheque from the government. Insanity has its payoffs. Rachael doesn't seem the type, though. Tia imagines that when she's well – which, she supposes, is now, seeing as she is once again free – she takes boudoir photos or makes jewellery. Maybe she's a graphic designer or a filmmaker and she sits at a fancy computer wearing big headphones, creating magical images with a million clicks of her mouse. She's an artist, Tia is sure of it. She makes beautiful things. Probably. Tia can't know. How to know? Nobody here would give out her information, and, Tia has to admit, if Rachael wanted to keep in touch, she could have given Tia her number, an address.

*

Tia's mother takes her out for a breath of freedom to buy toothpaste, deodorant, tampons, as if Tia is once again a teenager still living at home.

'And yarn, Mom, I need yarn.' She writes 'family pass' under 'Reason' in the sign-out book.

'I don't have the energy to make a big trip out of this, Tia.' Yvonne crosses her arms and scans the unit, uncomfortable as always with the psych ward.

'Just one roll, or whatever you call it,' says Tia in the elevator. 'I'm learning to knit.' She started that morning, at recreational therapy.

Lucky for Yvonne, they find acrylic yarn at the drugstore. Tia reaches for the brightest colours, Halloween orange and a royal blue not unlike Caveman's hospital gown.

'It's garish,' her mother says.

Tia's excitement turns into irritation and, inexplicably, nausea. 'Can you find me a bathroom?' she says, hands covering her mouth.

Her mother takes the skeins from Tia and drops them into the basket. She puts her free arm around her daughter's shoulders. 'Okay, honey, let's go.'

Tia's stomach heaves and she gags. The overwhelm is too much. She doesn't trust herself to speak, to say, *No, please, I need a bathroom,* in case she throws up right here. She wriggles out of her mother's embrace and heads toward the tills. There will be a bathroom at the front, there must be.

She finds one and vomits violently, still unsure why it is that she's throwing up, and when a stranger opens the door because she's neglected to lock it, she waves her arm desperately at them, afraid, ashamed, angry, and all of it coming out of her body in this dirty, public space.

*

She is briefly almost grateful to get back to the ward – and then she learns that Rachael was discharged while she was out. She didn't even say goodbye. Maybe, Tia hopes, Rachael had tried to say goodbye only to find her friend gone. She could have left a note.

'It's not summer camp,' Riley says at supper the night after Rachael's departure. He saw Tia sitting despondent and alone and took pity. 'It's not like on the last day we all promise to be pen pals.'

The man might be batshit, but he has a point. Tia puts Rachael in a drawer she is considering putting another woman into, a drawer where you place things you would best be served to forget.

Chapter 17

Andrew visits once. To walk into that hospital willingly is to leap off a cliff. Sure, they said you were well and set you free. What if they were waiting for your return to set the real trap? What if they only meant you could leave if you never came back? Yet, here he is, a handful of weeks after his departure, coming in on his own power. A sane man in an insane place. He passes a familiar patient pacing the wheelchair ramp along the east side of the building. He does not know the man's name, does not know if the reason he recognizes the shambling figure – fifty-something, grizzled, a waft of body odour and cigarettes warbling in his wake – is because he is so generically crazy Andrew presumes he must know him. He shakes his head, gives the man a wide berth, and tries not to think any more on this. He will tire out his brain on these things and it is not even noon. The outside world is exhausting.

The ward reeks of Mr. Clean and burnt decaffeinated coffee. On its own, not the worst aroma, especially in a place often full of people who have forgotten what the words *personal hygiene* mean. The odour conjures three months of memories – things he never told Tia, like how despite contraindications for its use in schizophrenia, he was given seven rounds of ECT, like how he once put a fist into Lenny the security guard's face. He swallows the bile that collects at his tonsils. Then mouth-breathes, cuts off his sense of smell.

Big Bernadette is there, big as ever and locked to her wheeled chair behind the nurses' desk. Her ID disappears into valleys of cleavage as she hunches over a magazine. A quiet day. A quiet moment in the storm. He has arrived exactly on schedule – 10:30 a.m. Breakfast done and cleaned up and lunch an hour away. It will give them a chance to talk, but just a small one. He misses Tia, misses her when he walks, free, easily in street clothes that hang a stitch looser every week, misses her when he laughs at his mother's British jokes over a meal that was made for three people, not thirty. Does he miss her the most when he takes himself in his hand, fingers curled into 'O.K.' around the head of his cock, and brings himself to orgasm with images of her on top of him, under him, beside him? Or does this feel like the strongest missing because it is the missing he feels in the deepest parts of his gut? He knows this is lust, but love lives there, too. When he was a baby, nobody whispered to him, 'Andrew, when you grow up, you're going to fall in love in a madhouse.' But that is what has happened.

No one sits in the chairs near the nurses' station. A coterie of unfamiliar patients zone out in front of the TV. New inmates. Andrew peeks into the 'activity' room, which the patients call the quiet room because it is a good place to go if you are on the verge of sensory overload. The nurses label it the activity room because they keep CDs in there (and the necessary stereo to play them), and crayons, and sheets of paper covered with pen drawings done by former resident crazies. Wild, scary scenes depicting unknowable animals. Photocopied by nurse after nurse, for colouring, for adding to, for use as notepad for the patient who feels she must keep track of every med, every doctor, does not trust what is in the chart. Who is the patient who drew these? How long have the nurses been creating these handmade colouring books? It is possible, Andrew knows, that these drawings are all that remain of the artist.

Today in the quiet room, Bruce rests on the couch, legs hanging off the end, his bare feet and long toes catching sun. He catches Andrew's eye for a moment in acknowledgement, and then returns to his stare at the ceiling. Not asleep, but not wanting to be disturbed.

Tia writes at a cafeteria table pulled close to the wall of windows. Riley with her, doing puzzles or problems on a sheet of graph paper. Andrew approaches them slowly. Tia is not expecting him. He did not call ahead. He was not sure until he left that he was coming, and he considered turning around several times. Eventually, he told himself he could not leave her alone in there for the rest of her sentence, he had to see her, and he might as well visit now. Tell her what he had in mind. Give her something to look forward to.

Tia scribbles with her back facing her ward, his old ward. She writes as if she is alone at the table. This is not a social engagement. When Riley pauses, he looks off into a distance that does not include Tia. To Andrew, they could be two students drafting papers at a library. Riley must have borrowed – or been given – clothes from a patient or family member of a different social caste: grey sweatpants fitted at the waist and loose at the ankles, with a brand name tattooed across the back waistband, and a V-neck plum-coloured T-shirt, which fits him like someone who knows something about fashion picked it out. Riley has a surprising bulge in his biceps, a flat stomach. Andrew tucks in the tummy that presses against the buckle of his jeans. Tia, bent over the table so her nose almost touches the paper she scribbles on, looks ... He finds the word at the same moment Riley catches sight of him and knocks a sandalled foot against Tia's sneaker under the table. *Normal.* She looks normal.

Every time it happens, it astounds him. Even in himself. From being so sick he cannot conceive of making himself breakfast, let alone being in the world looking for a job, shaking his father's hand – the hand that held the door for the police officers carrying Andrew off to the hospital – watching sitcoms without wondering if messages lie encoded in the laugh track. Should he be surprised? Nearly a month has passed since he saw Tia. She came here to get well, and she has.

'Andrew!' She gathers the pages with one swift motion into a neat pile, sets it face down, pats it, and then rises.

They meet in a hug. Andrew's stomach meets hers at the same time as he registers breasts pressed into his sternum, a palm cupping his shoulder blade. She pulls away before they have fully reached each other, ends what has barely begun. Not cool, exactly, but not ...

It was a perfectly fine hug. He told himself he would have no expectations. *She* hugged him. That is something.

'What are you doing here?'

'I came to visit.' *Ta-dah!* he almost adds, because that is how he sounds. A magician opening the cabinet door, turning the mirror one full circle.

Tia looks at an imaginary watch on her wrist. 'Took you long enough.'

Could she have missed him? Riley remains fully enthralled with his pencil and his problems.

'I've been busy.'

Tia watches him as he says this, knows he lies. She knows he has stayed away for a reason. 'Don't worry about it,' she says. 'You had shit to do.'

They are having what an outsider would call an absolutely normal conversation. Euphemism piled on top of euphemism, trading half-meanings like marbles. A bright fire flares deep in his chest, under the spot her breasts touched when they hugged. On impulse, he winks. Tia's face cracks, the composure shifting on its foundation, and one eye scrunches further closed than the other as she smiles.

'This place is, as usual, a shithole. I don't blame you for not visiting. Riley here gets out tomorrow, probably.' Riley looks up at this. 'Come sit,' Tia says, and motions Andrew over.

'I can't stay long,' he says, feet rooted to the high-gloss cafeteria floor.

'Don't worry about it. Sit. For a minute?'

Tia returns to her chair. Does he imagine how she carefully places an elbow on the pile of papers she turned over when he arrived? Andrew unlocks his feet and sits beside Tia, across from Riley. Riley does the same with his scribblings: turns them face down. Crazy people. Not even worth asking about. He tells them – her – about how he got back into trade school, is once again on his way to his electrician's apprenticeship. He forfeited his last apprenticeship because he lost his noodle halfway through, and they recommended he repeat his last school session. It could have been worse. He tells them living back at home is not so bad. He says this mostly for Tia's benefit. When she gets out, she will have to do the same. This is a lie. What man wants to go from the psych ward to his parents' house?

Tia says something strange: she mentions a patient she met the day he left, a woman who stayed only briefly. Rachael.

'Rachael? Black? Huge ass?'

Tia leans back.

'Butt,' he corrects. 'Bigger butt.' That might have been rude.

'You know her?' She did not expect he would.

'Oh, yes. I met her my second time in.'

'Huh.' Tia focuses on something above his head and she blinks. She chews the inside of her cheek.

'I'm sorry you had to meet Rachael. She is in here often. It is not really surprising.'

He remembers Rachael suggesting they fuck in the quiet room. He could not get an erection – it was physically impossible given the cocktail he was on. The erection lived deep in his spine and somewhere in his primitive brain. For a moment. Until he shuddered. It was the only time he put hands on another patient and immediately he regretted it. He pushed against her shoulders and she grabbed for his hands.

She was strong, dug her fingers in. 'Don't be a fucking pussy.'

He wrenched his fingers free. Her nails left marks on the backs of his hands that he carried for days.

'Crazy bitch,' he said, face hot, that pressure in his groin something between wanting to come and being kicked in the sack.

'Andrew?' This from Tia, in front of him. 'Why sorry?'

Close that memory. 'Riley told you, did he not?' Riley registers his name being said but does not look up from his graph paper. 'She has a personality disorder.'

'No. That was – ' She stops.

'She is a classic case of histrionic personality disorder. She is a nutball, so she winds up here a lot. I hear. Like I said, I only met her the once.' He hopes the rush of blood he feels in his upper thighs cannot be detected on his face. He has not thought about Rachael in a while. Took her memory to bed with him on the outside a few times and then let that image disappear from the vault. In the end, she was too fucked up to be hot.

'That's what she said.'

'What?' He had disappeared again, into his head. Did he say something out loud?

'She told me about personality disorders. Not that one ...'

'Histrionic.'

'Not histrionic. Anyway ... ' Tia's face slackens.

'You made friends,' Andrew says, comprehending.

'Yeah.'

'I'm sorry.'

'This fuckin' place.' Tears stifle her words.

'I am sorry,' Andrew says again, reaching out. When he touches Tia's hand, nothing happens. No surge of electricity from one body to another. She does not pull back either. She lets him rest his hand there. Riley's gaze shifts a couple of inches.

Yeah, buddy, you watch. I am taking this girl with me.

'It is a thing with people like that,' Andrew says. 'They are charmers.'

Tia coughs out the tears hanging in the back of her throat and pulls her hand away.

Could've kept your trap shut about Rachael, you twit.

Could have. Should have. Nothing he can do about it now.

There are things he chooses not to say: How he has been to the bank to ask about getting a line of credit so he can move out, get his own apartment. How he has been looking at apartments big enough for two. How when he mentioned Tia's name to his mother for the umpteenth time, her eyebrows went up and he did not correct the look.

The whole time – only half an hour – all he can think is, *So this is normal. Normal.* Tia pretty as ever – the romantic in him wants to say gorgeous, but Tia is not gorgeous – and Riley friendly. Not an imaginary lover or fantastic invention anywhere in sight. Do they feel it, too? Not yet. They will. The spark is gone. They do not tell you that when you sign in, but it is part of the agreement. We will make you better, we will guide you back to the right side of reality and once you are here, we will close the door. Reality is waiting for you. Your room is ready. Here, would you like a travel-sized bottle of Get Your Life Back on Track or maybe a single-use Appointment with a Social Worker? Sorry, we simply do not have the resources to provide you with further help. Good luck. Go on. *Go!*

He shakes Riley's hand, hugs Tia. 'I would like to spend time with you once you have been released.' He has practised this all week.

'I would like that,' is all she says, without more than the average pause for thinking, everything so suddenly average he wants to scream. He hooks clenching fingers through a belt loop and breathes through the mini-explosion in his brain. Focuses on her words.

She said yes, you stupid git.

Yes, yes, she did.

He smiles, nods to Riley, his typical formality returning to comfort him in this moment of anger, and with a wave that includes them both, he turns away and heads for the elevators. He disappears into his thoughts, replaying the conversation, and walks right into a chair. The corner crowbars into the flesh on the side of his thigh, a charley horse quick in its stead. Caveman sits there, curled into a ball, face buried between knees, only his ears exposed.

'Shit, mate. Sorry.'

Caveman looks up and makes eye contact. Andrew cannot remember having been this close to Caveman, ever seeing the man's eyes. Buried deep in sockets surrounded by spiderwebs of wrinkles and deeply tanned skin, they blaze a colour he would, if pressed, describe as green. Green like a moraine lake, like the grey-green shale that crawls up either side of the Trans-Canada Highway through the Rockies. It comes to him: jasper. The rock that gave the park its name.

'Got sick of the laundry room?' Andrew says. It is an inappropriate thing to say, verging on unkind. It is just that he and Caveman have never spoken. Caveman prefers the white noise of the dryer and the microwave to human interaction.

Thankfully, the man does not seem to mind. Or perhaps he did not hear. 'Be careful.'

Andrew steps back. Caveman's hand appears on his wrist like it has always been there and Andrew jerks. Caveman's grip does not give. His fingers, calluses and bone, find the space between wrist and the base of Andrew's thumb. He squeezes. Andrew feels it in his knees, the right side of his lower back. He shrinks.

'Careful. Yes?' The man's blue-green eyes don't look so pretty now. His hair, brown and grey and coarse, wraps around his head like a mane and joins at some indeterminate point with his beard.

With a measured mixture of docility and sincerity, Andrew replies, 'Yes.'

Caveman's fingers loosen immediately and a shadow falls over his expression. His head disappears between his knees, and he buries his ears, too; now nothing but the wiry salt-and-pepper puff of his hair can be seen. Andrew glances back. Tia and Riley have returned to their pages. *What is she writing?* he allows himself to wonder, and then carries on, descends via the elevator, exits the building. It has started raining. The air washes through his nostrils, fresh and clean.

Thank you, Caveman, he thinks. *At least one of you still knows what it means to be crazy.*

Chapter 18

Night after night, for the first time in years, Tia awakens with her body in knots. A nurse or Moira, her roommate, stands over the bed. Sometimes they pin her down. She tries to scream, can't. Screams and can't stop. The hands feel like the tentacles of a thousand furious octopuses. In the moment between sleep and consciousness, familiar images: the steel-trap mouth of teeth, row upon row of knife-blade incisors, ready to gobble her up. The terror breaks into wakefulness and the images scatter. She is left only with dread and anxiety spilling out of her.

At her regular meetings with the Irish shrink, they discuss the dreams, which started the night after Rachael left.

'Sorry, doc, I can't really remember the dreams.' She feels off, badly slept. Talking about the terrors is like talking about someone else's memories.

'This is normal, from what I've read,' O'Shea says.

He tells her that night terrors don't have a clear medical explanation, that they come and go. He admits it's unusual for her to have them again after so long. He admits he doesn't have a fucking clue. Something in Tia gloats, this part of her the expert cannot explain.

After several bad mornings, it occurs to Tia there is someone who can help her. She asks O'Shea if she can consult with someone outside the hospital.

'Outside?'

'Yeah. Another doctor. Well, sort of.' Ira. 'Not a medical doctor. I think he has a PhD in psychology.'

'Why do you want to see this person?'

A psychologist can't even prescribe meds, O'Shea's probably thinking. *What good is that?*

'I did therapy with him when I was a kid. He knew a lot about dreams. Sleep stuff.' *He's a regular fucking Freud, Dr. O'Shea*, she wants to say.

'You received psychotherapy as a child?' O'Shea opens her chart. He writes less in it every time. He has her all figured out. He no longer needs to take notes. This, however, is new.

She has had many opportunities to provide this information, but each time she chose not to. Incomplete medical history. Things they didn't need to know. 'I had night terrors. My parents sent me to this child psychologist, this sleep specialist.'

'Oh, well, if he's a child psychologist, he may not be willing to see you. That was years ago. Is he still practising?'

'I have no idea. Can you, like, do a consult or something?'

'You've been watching too much TV, Tia,' O'Shea says with a laugh. *Asshole.*

'You would need a referral. It would take a couple of weeks. He'll likely have a wait-list. It could be quite a while.'

Because I'm in a rush?

O'Shea waits. Tia stares. Finally, he says, 'I can't bring him in to see you, no. It doesn't work that way.'

'Fine. Forget it.'

'Tia.'

'No, really. Forget it. I'm sure it'll pass. Like it did the first time.'

'You're probably right.' Just like that, O'Shea's calm and composed robotic self is back.

Tia started seeing Ira the child psychologist in Grade 1. By January of Grade 3, they had a regular appointment. Always a weekday, mid-morning, so Tia got to leave school. Maybe that's why she liked going so much. The kids asked her where she went; she chose to be vague. Cultivated the mystery of having a problem. Like Shilo, who came back from Christmas break with glasses. Like Daniel, who dropped like a felled tree during a game of grounders and spasmed. The children watched, enthralled, some tittering, some afraid, some, like Tia, totally, shamefully engrossed. Daniel did a presentation for class later that year about epilepsy, and they all tried not to smirk. They did not understand, could not. Ira was Tia's epilepsy, her bad eyes. Word got around.

'You're crazy,' said Shilo. She hadn't spoken to Tia in weeks.

'No, I'm not.' Tia wished for the quip that wouldn't come.

'Yeah, you are. You're seeing a therapist. My mom told me. And that means you're crazy.' Shilo, a girl who had mastered the quip, turned around and left her once-friend blank-faced, staring and alone.

Tia fought the tears. Fell against the cement wall of their elementary, slid, let her sweatpants-clad bum hit gravel, and cried. Wanted Shilo to see. Wanted Shilo to know.

The next memory springs from sometime later, deep into March. She stood outside the school waiting for her ride to see Ira. It was sometimes her mother who came, sometimes her father. She preferred her father. Sometimes he'd get her ice cream before taking her back to school. Or they'd dawdle, and she wouldn't have to deal with the latest lunch-hour drama on the playground. That day, no one came. She stood and stood. Didn't want to check with an adult inside the school in case in that moment her mother came and was forced to wait for her. She didn't have a watch. Eventually Mr. Astrander the janitor came by. He smiled his usual smile and his bald pate gleamed under the clear winter sun. Tia couldn't feel her toes. She asked the time. More than forty-five minutes had passed. She had missed her appointment. She started breathing fast. Ira! Ira was expecting her. There was a charge for missed appointments! She said this in an eight-year-old's shriek, this bit about the missed appointments, to Mr. Astrander. He took her to the principal's office.

'Your mother called me a few days ago, Tia,' said the principal. She patted Tia's hand and eyed the clock.

No one had thought to tell Tia, and the memo didn't make it to Tia's teacher. No one had thought to look for her when she missed class as usual. When Tia got home she screamed – a scream that was put to a stop with a flat palm against her bare backside.

'I told you,' Tia's mother said, as Tia sat on her hands at the kitchen table, buttocks stinging. 'I told you this morning. No more appointments.'

Tia was no longer allowed to say, 'No, you didn't.' That's what had gotten her the spanking. You never tell your mother she's wrong. Ever.

'Your problem, Tia, is that you don't listen.'

'I liked Ira ...' Tia tried, as loud as she dared, a whisper of a whisper.

Her mother heard and didn't reply. She returned to her work at the counter. A half-hour later, dinner was served, and Tia's mother and father talked of the boring things they always talked about, none of which stuck anywhere in Tia's memory. Then, like here with Dr. O'Shea, Tia's problems were brushed aside, sweetly and easily, like sand off a stoop.

Now, their meeting over, O'Shea stands. He gives her the slightest of nods. His mind's already somewhere else, another patient, his wife at home. He walks away and leaves Tia sitting, staring after him.

✳

She chose to put Rachael in a drawer, but she won't forget Andrew. Can't. Especially since he visited. Each day her thoughts of him remain and each day she wonders. They're less an ocean devouring her and more a warm blanket she can pull over her shoulders when she wants comfort. A soft ebb of *What if?* followed by the flow of an easy, unpressured *Maybe*. Maybe.

Maybe what?

'Tia?' O'Shea's voice comes from somewhere. There, across from her. Another day, another meeting. Her focus has finally returned, after being sucked from her – by trauma, by drugs with names she cannot pronounce. These days, she is more *on* than when she was well, a drug side effect that no one calls a side effect. Her conversations with O'Shea, however, verge on soporific. Worse, she gets the impression he feels the same way. God, what a horrible job.

'Sorry.'

O'Shea cuts a head shake before it becomes full-on. 'No problem,' he says. It's not like he can say, *No one's forcing you to be here, Tia*, or, *Look, if you don't want to do this, we don't have to* … as if he were some superintendent in a made-for-TV movie. 'I was asking you about the terrors. They've disappeared. As quickly as they came.'

'Looks like.'

'Well,' he says, chuffed. 'Good.'

'I couldn't have done it without you, Dr. O'Shea.'

Magically, O'Shea doesn't hear Tia's sarcasm, even though it's honey-thick. Shock hits her. Guilt. Christ, now she's got human feelings again. Being crazy had its perks. This real-life business is one bit of bullshit after another.

'Oh well, I didn't do much. In this case. Dreams are not my forte.' He's smiling, face lit up like a dozen birthday candles burning.

'Well, still,' Tia says. She searches for something approaching sincerity. Where did her ability to dismiss O'Shea the domain-master go, her ability to guide this treatment as if she knew best? If she sticks around long enough, she's liable to like him. Well, maybe not. She might disdain him less, appreciate the hell he must endure most days.

She used to be a nice person. She remembers that. Before here, before Pacifique. The kind of person who gave her friends money, who stood alongside her mother for hours in the kitchen at Christmas and Thanksgiving. The kind of person who said, all the bloody time, 'No, it's fine. Don't worry about it.' She feels the edge she brought in like armour softening, and her dislike of O'Shea retreating, but she will never go back to being Miss Nice. Somebody was always trying to get something from her. Once it was a roommate short on rent – eventually it became Pacifique. And then O'Shea, or Rachael, or even Andrew. Best to assume the worst in people. Then you're not disappointed.

'Pacifique isn't real.' She doesn't blurt it. She doesn't yell or scream or leap onto her chair and shout it from there, the closest she can get to a rooftop.

O'Shea waits. Meets her gaze. His poker face belies nothing. He doesn't reach for his pen to scribble the good news into her chart.

'She isn't real. She never was.'

'Okay,' O'Shea says, soft and measured and emotionless like a first responder on the scene of a grisly accident. Tia imagines him in a navy-blue uniform like the moustache man who pulled her into the ambulance after the bike crash. *Hold still*, he would say. *This is going to hurt.* Because this is the easy part, really, this and everything that's come before, and she knows he would say so if he were less professional. *Welcome to your new life, Tia*, he would say if he were a different man. *Your new life alone. I promise you it won't be nearly as fun as life with Pacifique.*

One less person to disappoint her.

O'Shea doesn't say anything, doesn't offer her the words she thinks he would like to say. She nods, anyway, accepts what is unspoken, and sighs as the fluorescent lights flicker above them. Tia watches the lamps dim and stutter back to something approaching brilliance. O'Shea doesn't appear to notice. She squints against the glare that doesn't come. She opens her eyes, wide, and the beams overhead no longer burn her irises. Everything lit and visible and nothing at all too much to bear.

Chapter 19

Rachael asked about the note Pacifique wrote, the one she left on the bed the morning she went to find the metallic green bicycle. Rachael wondered where it was. Tia crawled through memories and story. She decided she had kept it, that she must have, and scoured her hospital room. Her mother had brought a houseplant (a smart move, better than flowers), and Tia asked for a second. She tore pages out of magazines and taped them to the wall. She stuck her colouring up, too, tiny art prints, her own gallery. She made a nameplate for the room door and put both her and Moira's names on it. Moira, a squat woman who only ever spoke once – to tell Tia not to put her name on the door – sat most days on the edge of her bed. For hours. Tia never learned her diagnosis, decided it must be some crippling depression. A blackness Tia could not fathom. Moira didn't get visitors either. What light could there be for a person like that in a place like this? The biggest part of your day the moment the nurse comes in – not because she brings pills, because clearly nothing works – but because she's human. Alive. Has a voice.

Tia took offence when Moira told her to take her name off the door. She folded the sheet of construction paper in half so only *Tia* showed. Later, she understood. Tia's desire to lay claim to a place, her room, a piece of mania she brought with her. A name on the door says, *Here I am, here. Find me inside. Yes, I live in a lunatic asylum.* Tia's door the only one with anything on it, not a single other patient wanting to announce this information. They were in that respect all saner than she was.

But Tia had a powerful ulterior motive: Pacifique. How would Pacifique find her if she was faced with two U-shaped hallways of door after plain door, faded salmon in colour and flush with the faded salmon walls, without even doorknobs to break the pattern? A person could get lost looking down that hallway. Even after Tia realized Pacifique wasn't coming, she left the name. It was a tiny bit of routine she had created for herself in this place.

In her room: piles of paper; two plants; a clutch of street clothes; fancy, strong-smelling bath things her mother had brought because isn't that what you bring your daughter in a psych ward? Tia could not find the note. She didn't have it. It must still be at her house. When she cast her mind to her house, she imagined a tornado. Her mother had told her several times the place was a disaster. Tia had apparently taken over parts of the house besides her own room. Esther's drawers of sewing materials dumped on the living room floor. Piles made with these things, piles that made no sense to Tia's mother or anyone else. Tia's room a mountain surrounded by four walls, everything Tia owned pulled from the wall, the dresser, the closet, under the bed, and put in the room's centre, an attempt to find, what, clues?

'The blinds, Tia, even the blinds,' Tia's mother told her. 'You took them off the windows and dumped them on top of everything else.'

Tia stifled a chuckle. Her mother glared.

'Oh, c'mon, Mom, you're exaggerating.'

'I am not.'

It was just that Tia didn't remember. She remembered canvassing every restaurant Pacifique might go to, asking her roommates, asking neighbours, even asking her classmates. When Rachael asked about the note, it was because it could be used as proof of Pacifique's existence, one way or the other. And if the house was as her mother described it, she would never find the note there.

When Tia didn't find it in her things, she got thinking. Thinking about the way a dream fades no matter how exciting or strange. How everything erodes over time. How even though you know it wasn't real, a part of you still wants to remember. It broke the rules, but she wanted to remember, to record what she could recall of Pacifique. Wasn't so much of her pain, day in and day out, caused by the sheer effort required to put this story together? It was exhausting being confused all the time. What if she wrote it down and then moved on?

She wrote and wrote. Everything she could remember. Asked Riley for clarification on points she knew she had shared with him when she first arrived and had since forgotten. He had an excellent memory, a facility with details. Riley had even taken to working alongside her when she wrote. She kept it from everyone else. When O'Shea told her he'd seen her writing, she said she was keeping notes for a book she was thinking of writing about this place.

O'Shea smiled, attempted to lean back in his stiff-backed chair, and said, 'People say that.'

People say that and don't do it, he meant. Fair enough. She wasn't going to do it. She hoped to forget she had ever been here.

Andrew couldn't know. The pages admitted one thing, and she had said another.

If Rachael had stayed, Tia might have told her about the writing. Rachael had once said, 'Always keep with you what came before. Never leave any of it behind.' She'd meant it more as a lesson for the mentally ill, as a lesson for someone who measured her life in hospital stays. Still, Tia thought she would approve of the pages.

Andrew, she knew, would not.

✳

O'Shea decertifies Tia on a Tuesday. They sit where they sat the first time they met. Tia had felt close to normal in that moment two months ago, speaking with the psychiatrist, studying the pubic-like curls that carpeted his skull. For the first time in she couldn't remember how long, she had slept. She spoke to a nurse about 'checking out' – the term brings a hard smile to the corners of her mouth now, the hospital that morning just a place to stay the night – and the nurse said she would need to speak to a psychiatrist.

'Wow. It's amazing what a good night's sleep will do,' she said to the doctor. Then she said something – she can't remember now exactly what it was – about going home.

'Do you think you can leave?' O'Shea asked.

She ignored the tone in his voice. 'Of course I can leave,' she said. She turned in her chair and hooked a thumb over her shoulder. 'The elevators are right over there.'

The previous night had already started to fade, but she remembered the elevators. What goes up must come down. Mustn't it?

Scribble scribble went the doctor and the meeting ended. 'Certifiable,' wrote the doctor in her chart. Unfit for human consumption. Stamp: CRAZY. It was a nurse who told her the bad news.

This time, months later and perhaps because it's nicer to give than take away, O'Shea proffers her freedom himself. Just like that, she can go.

✳

Her mother comes on discharge day, three days later. All that Tia has acquired fits in three plastic 'patient belongings' bags. Orthopedic pillow under the right arm; Flopsy, a once-rabbit long bereft of its ears, under the left. She has been told to check in at the nurses' desk before she leaves and she does, her mother at her side. She gets the same discharge talk everyone does. After overhearing it dozens of times while seated in her spot of choice, she could recite it to herself. She doesn't. She stands, quiet and compliant, and allows the nurse to do her job. When it comes to the meds, there isn't much to say. The doctors say her problem was brain injury–induced psychosis. No faulty wiring or chemistry to blame. No pill that can cure her, they say. *Cure* her word, of course, not theirs. She will leave the hospital with an antipsychotic she knows she will shortly stop taking. She and O'Shea went over the details earlier. The more important script is the lorazepam, *pro re nata*. For the anxiety when it comes.

'And the things from your cubby,' says the nurse, perusing a checklist Tia assumes will live in her chart for eternity. Or until some disgruntled inmate burns the fucking place down.

It's not until the nurse returns with something in her hands after twenty seconds out of sight in the med room that Tia, still quiet and compliant, computes the nurse's words.

'What cubby?' she risks.

Then she recognizes what the woman holds: Tia's wallet, house keys, one of Esther's particularly pretty safety pins, and a red leather belt Tia forgot she owned. The pin might be better called a diaper pin, big enough to pierce through several folds of the softest cotton, adorned with a cornflower-blue head. The nurse places the items on the counter and makes four swift marks on the checklist. Each item logged, each item returned.

Nobody mentioned a cubby. When Tia needed money for the coffee shop, she asked for her debit card, and when she returned, she gave it back. Later she used the money her mom gave her and kept that in her room. She would have left her debit card at the hospital if they hadn't reminded her, and the rest of her wallet's contents. Plus Esther's pin and the belt. *A danger to herself or others.*

She threads the belt through her pant loops, and it unfurls in her hand like parchment. She goes for the familiar, well-used hole. Her body resists. Damn antipsychotics, lard in pill form. She settles on a more comfortable notch and reaches for the wallet. She counts the money, two small bills, change jingling in the zippered pouch. She barely remembers the wallet, let alone how much money may or may not have been in it. Fights the notion that Big Bernadette stole from her.

Then she sees it. The note. It's just a folded piece of notebook paper. She knows it immediately: Pacifique's note. Tia's chest shudders, her heart beating too fast. Her palms go hot and slick. The lights flicker, too bright. She steels herself against the blush that creeps northward from her armpits.

'Is it okay if I use the bathroom? My bathroom? I mean, before I go?' she asks in her most normal of normal voices.

'Of course, Tia.' The nurse doesn't even look at her.

Tia's mother turns with a sigh, which Tia answers with, 'I'll be quick. Really have to pee.'

She wants to run, thinks running might actually be the appropriate thing to do, people run when they're in a rush and her mother is waiting, but nobody runs on the ward and imagine if this is the moment it all becomes clear and they notice and take it all away from her because she is running. So, a fast walk. One foot in front of the other, the wallet slipped in the back pocket of her jeans, the note folded and invisible in her palm.

She pushes into her room – not her room anymore; in fact, someone has already put the bed in its original position in the corner instead of where she had it, under the window – and, while crossing the invisible dividing line, runs into Moira. Her body a statue. Moira, who never does anything but sit on the edge of her bed.

'Oh my god, Moira, I'm sorry.'

Tia reaches for the woman, who recoils.

'Sorry,' Tia says again. Stars float at the periphery of her vision.

Moira doesn't move, remains as still as she always was when perched on her plastic mattress.

'I'm just going to the bathroom one last time. Don't want to have to pee while driving home.'

Why would she say that? To a chronic like Moira? Moira's face doesn't change. *Is she deaf?* Tia can't believe it didn't occur to her before. She waits another beat, then two, and still the woman doesn't react. Then she blinks. Once, then a second time.

Later, Tia will think back on this moment and be sure something appeared in Moira's face, a tiny whisper of the future.

Tia disappears into the bathroom. Presses her back against the door, closes it. She sits on the toilet seat, rocks a moment from side to side to get the creak she knows can be heard in the room beyond, and turns on the tap.

In her palm, the letter has wilted. For a moment, she envisions the page crumbling to dust like a pressed flower. The sweat from her hand has softened the paper, and it opens easily under her fingers.

Dearest Tia,
I have gone on a treasure hunt. I will find you. Have a good day at school.
Love, Pacifique
p.s. You are a light, the sun.

The handwriting spikes across the page on a slight angle. Neat and tidy but written by someone in a rush. Someone running out. Or someone not quite right in the head. The hand is pretty and familiar, its *y*'s angular, its *i*'s dotted just so. Familiar and pretty and undeniably her own.

Part 2

Chapter 20

Time spent sane passes, and passes some more, and one day *it's months, more than a year, since you were crazy.* Tia finds herself caught in thoughts that carry her to places she doesn't often allow herself to go. She settles into a kneel, lays dirt-encrusted hands in her lap, and forgets for a moment that she came out to weed and check on the tomatoes. They're still green, mostly, but some of the smallest ones are bright red enough to eat, and she pauses, wondering if she should pick them or leave them. She's no gardener, never has been, it's Andrew's mother, Shirley, who's the expert. With this uncertainty ahead of her, her brain opens and lets in other things. She puts one hand on the ground and taps off the days into the grass with her fingers. Forty-two days between the accident and admission. Fifty-nine days certified. One hundred and one crazy days. And sane? Tia leans back, scans the clouds, visualizes a calendar flipping over. Closing in on a year and a half. She shivers and clears her throat against the sudden prickle of nausea in her stomach.

Tomatoes. She'll take them, the small ones. They're perfect now. They come off the vine with a life-affirming pop and go into her mouth with a similar sound.

So much for the salad – but Andrew doesn't care for her salads, anyway. In the honeymoon period, he tried. Did a lot of things he didn't like doing. Eating vegetables, unfortunately, one of those things. The more she pushes, the more he refuses. He knows he's gaining weight, and she knows, and it is one of several unspoken things they tiptoe around. The other morning, she poked one of his love handles while he stood shaving at the sink wearing only a towel. He grabbed her hand, squeezed. Popped Tia's knuckles.

'Ow!' she said, and squirmed.

He released her hand and had the decency to look a little contrite. Tia scowled and left him alone. He closed the door behind her.

Since then, she has not again caught him undressed. What is this distance between them? Stress? Not enough time at home? Too much? She doesn't have the proper tools to fix whatever is the matter. It was easy, in the beginning. New relationships always are. She and Andrew shared something nobody else could even begin to understand. That bond is still there, but real life, the outside world, it gets in the way. It had to, eventually.

Tia stands and presses her fingers into her thigh. Visualizes the calendar again. Can't come up with how long it has been since they last had sex. She shakes the numbers, the dates, from her head and pushes through the apartment-building doors, climbs the stairs to their second-floor suite. Inside it, Andrew sits with his back to her, slope-shouldered at his computer. Tia clamps her teeth, finds a stray piece of tomato skin.

'It's too nice out to game,' she says, her voice familiar but not because it's her own. She swallows the tomato bit. 'We should go for a walk.' Her mother's voice. That's what it is. She clears her throat.

Silence from Andrew. One hand hovers over the keyboard.

Tia glides through the tension in the living room. Finds her partner's shoulders. A jerk of surprise, a holding on, and then, thankfully, a release. She digs in, trapezius and scalene and sternocleidomastoid moving under her fingers. She knows these muscles from study; she knows his muscles from time. Many back rubs. The man is tense.

'It's okay,' she says, and although she intends it lightly, she still hears something measured, calculated in her tone. She kisses Andrew on the cheek. 'Never mind.'

She means it; she no longer needs or wants him to walk with her. At this moment all she wants is to be alone again – but why does it sound like she's angry? She steps away, intent for their bathroom so she can wash the dirt from her hands and knees. Andrew grabs her wrist. This time she jerks. He pulls her hand to his mouth, puts his dry lips to the palm, turns it over, kisses the first and second knuckles.

He looks up, her Andrew, perfectly fine, everything just fine, and says, 'I love you.' Sure, he says it with a hint of sadness, but he is a sad man, in a similar way that she is sad. That many people are sad.

'I love you, too,' she says, and finally her voice lacks any tension or pretense. 'So much,' she adds, and he releases her.

He turns to his computer and she turns for their bedroom and everything is, once again, brightly forgotten.

Chapter 21

In the aftermath of his third hospital stay, Andrew saw his psychiatrist, Dr. Benson, twice a week. Then weekly. Then, for many months, they saw each other biweekly and for only half an hour. Victory. He knew not to hold it to standards like that, knew that any victory can be followed by a loss, that the strongest emperors always fall, often due to their own hubris. He tried not to be proud. Not to revel in wellness. He tried, and he failed. Now he pays the price. He cannot remember when it happened, when Benson looked at her calendar and told him she could fit him in the following week. Or when he asked if he could have more time next appointment, did she have a forty-five-minute spot? Did he ask for that or did she suggest it? He cannot remember. He has an appointment tomorrow, for an hour, and he remembers having an hour-long appointment recently. It must have been last week. Did they meet for forty-five minutes at any point? Maybe she never said forty-five minutes. He has it written down. It is in his book. He has it written down. *Yes, there.* Tomorrow, correct, he remembered that right. One hour. And then, last week. He searches through the scribblings on the pages, most of them unrelated to things he has to do because he is not the kind of person to have a lot of social engagements, he never has been. Yes, nested between 'light bulbs for Tia' and 'soap: phosphates?' is last week's one-hour appointment with Dr. Benson. There, proof. Weekly visits each an hour long. Is victory truly victory if it does not last?

The headache slices deep into his cerebrum and flares like a sun burning out. He clutches his head with his right hand, grabs the desk with his left, and curls over. He presses against the eyeball under his palm, and just like that the ache disappears. He waits, hunched. It doesn't return. Only then does he risk taking a breath. All is well. He drops his hands, straightens, and a black curtain dusted with stars rushes in from all sides.

※

'Oh, sweetheart, you've hit your head.'

Tia's voice is clear and familiar, but it comes through several layers of space and time, from across the room or down the street.

'No, no, it's okay, don't move. Relax.'

He sees table legs on hardwood skating toward the baseboards, dust bunnies making friends with the tangle of cords under his desk.

'I'm here,' she says, waving a hand in his peripheral vision before placing it on his upper arm. 'You stood up too fast. Your blood pressure must be low.'

'You saw me?' What did she see? Was she just standing there?

'Yeah, you were bent over, and when you stood up, you went straight back down.'

Not a touch of worry in her voice. In fact, the opposite of worry. He rolls over against the resistance provided by her hand and says, 'It's not funny.'

Tia cannot stifle the laugh now. It hiccups out of her. 'I'm sorry,' she hoots, and covers her mouth. The floorboards beneath them vibrate with her laughter.

'I hit my head,' he says. Weariness rolls over him.

Tia stops vibrating. 'You're right. And that's why I'm going to help you up and we're going to go to the clinic. You know how I am about head injuries.'

Tia guides him into the fetal position, to sitting cross-legged with his head bowed, to a chair, to his feet.

'How do you feel?' she asks. She faces him, hands on his arms. He knows why she is always fully booked in the student clinic at the massage school. If she chooses to, she can make you feel like you are the only person in the world. Right now, she chooses him. It feels good.

'Fine,' he answers. It is true. He feels fine. He remembers being irritated, but at what?

Whatever it was, a voice tells him from somewhere deep inside his body – maybe under the shoulder blade, which twinges. Did he hit that on the way down? – whatever it was, *it'll come back.*

Chapter 22

'Tiiiaaaa.' Somebody hisses from the other side of the book stack.

Tia peers through a gap in the nearest books. Isn't that where the other person always is in a library?

'Tia!' A woman stands waving and smiling at the end of the row. 'Tia! Hi! It's me. Rachael!'

How could she forget Rachael? She designed herself to be unforgettable. 'I know,' Tia finally manages. What in hell is Rachael doing here?

Rachael approaches, doesn't stop, even when she has most definitely stepped into Tia's bubble. *No boundaries*, Andrew said once.

'Sooo,' Rachael says, glancing over her shoulder and then back, straight into Tia's face. 'How's Pacifique?'

Tia can't help the gasp that comes out of her, so surprised to hear the name. And then, immediately, she feels angry. *You bitch* is what she wants to say. The words appear in front of her like a line on a teleprompter. She won't say it. Not here. Not to this woman who will likely twist the words into something else. 'Um …' is all she gets out.

Rachael doesn't help her. Just stares. That same smile plastered on her face. She looks positively thrilled.

'What do you mean?' Tia says. It feels like capitulation, admitting she's confused, but she doesn't know how else to get Rachael to go away or stop grinning like they've both won the lottery.

'You do remember me, right, from Ian Charles?'

Part of her wants to look around for the cameras. 'Of course I remember you, Rachael.'

'Good. Oh, I've thought about you a bunch since then. I was hoping I'd run into you. And here you are, at my library.' *Her* library.

Tia waits. There is nothing to say.

'So, Pacifique.'

'Is not real.' The words come now. Her fingertips buzz and her heart pounds with anxiety. Her cheeks burn with anger.

The smile finally cracks. Something approaching a frown etches its way across Rachael's lipsticked mouth. Sephora #20, Wanted Red, Tia recalls. The colour Rachael wears. What a stupid thing to remember.

'Oh.' Rachael looks away. 'That's what they convinced you of, hey?' she says, all excitement stricken from her voice.

Fight-or-flight hormones course through Tia's veins. '*I* convinced myself of that.'

Rachael squints with something that is either disappointment or disbelief.

No, that isn't right.

Tia can almost hear the *Oh, really?* written across Rachael's face. She imagines the balled fist at her side hitting Rachael somewhere near the left temple. 'It wasn't about convincing.' Every word an arrow she wants to fire into that pretty face. 'Pacifique isn't real. She never was. I had to come to terms with that. You know, like, stop being fucking crazy.'

Rachael backs up two steps. Tia feels suddenly able to breathe. Until Andrew told her the story of Rachael attempting to seduce him in the activity room, Tia hadn't thought that sex on the inside was possible. As much as she still has trouble believing that Rachael would proposition Andrew – she would go for men with money, men with wives, older men, Tia imagines – she does believe that Rachael charmed her way into Tia's good books, that most of their friendship was a manipulation.

Yeah, I can stand up for myself, she thinks. *Try your tricks now.* Her entire body vibrates.

'What about the letter?' Rachael's voice is low, almost a whisper, like she just realized they're in a place best suited for quiet conversations.

At first, Tia doesn't know what she means. She's briefly distracted from her jittering body. For a moment. 'Oh!' She laughs. 'That! I found it. It was in my cubby, behind the nurses' desk.'

'And?' Rachael leans forward.

'It was fake.'

'Fake?'

Tia shakes her head to find the words. She consciously inhales, counteracting the high-chested, anxious breathing. 'I mean, I wrote it. It was in my handwriting. Crazy, right? Yeah.' The urge to punch her once-friend – not a friend, no: a woman who made her think they were friends – has faded as quickly as it appeared.

'Huh,' says Rachael, her mouth going slack with the questions she no longer has on the tip of her tongue. Then she snatches Tia's gaze again. 'Do you have a notebook? Something you write in?'

'What do you mean? Why?'

'You do, right?'

'Sure. I have a daytimer. But I should go.'

'One minute, Tia. Humour me. Then I'll leave.'

Tia recognizes this part of Rachael. She knew her once, for a handful of days, in a psych ward. 'I don't really want to think about the hospital.'

It's true. She doesn't. Although now she's not sure she wants Rachael to go. That's probably Rachael working her charm.

'Of course,' Rachael says. 'I'm sorry, I sometimes forget, 'cause I've been in so many times, and you only the once, it's different for you.'

'I'd say.'

Rachael flinches. 'The book. Your daytimer. May I? I'm not gonna steal it.'

'I didn't ... I wasn't ...'

Rachael puts out a hand. Tia shrugs off her backpack, opens the zipper, and finds the small book. Rachael snags it.

'Hey!' Tia reaches.

Rachael steps out of range, snaps open the book, scans for a second, and points at something. 'Is that your writing?'

Tia glances. 'Of course it is.'

Rachael rifles through pages, points at something else. 'And this?'

Tia doesn't bother looking. 'Yes, of course. Nobody else writes in that. It's all mine.'

Rachael bookmarks the page with a finger and goes back to the first entry, which, on second look Tia sees is an appointment several months back with a massage client.

'This,' Rachael says, pointing to the appointment, 'and this. Are they identical?'

Of course! Tia wants to scream. The second notation is more recent, about a month ago, a note about a robin's egg she found on the sidewalk. She can't now remember the moment, but it must have made an impression. No. They're not identical. They're both her writing, of course, but not copies. The appointment letters created more carefully, blocky. The note about the egg a scrawl, a messy cursive.

Rachael snaps the book shut and Tia jumps. 'That's all. I'll leave you alone. I'm sorry.'

Rachael drops the daytimer. Tia grabs it before it hits the ground. Rachael beelines for the end of the aisle. 'No, Rachael, you don't understand. Just fucking wait, goddammit.' Somewhere behind or beside her, an offended *shhht.*

Rachael disappears around the shelf. Tia finds her feet and stumbles after her, catches herself, turns back for her bag, then leaves it, she'll be back, she needs to catch Rachael. She bursts onto the street, and the sun rakes away her vision. She blinks against the whiteness, the milliseconds crawling. When the square outside the library comes into shape, nothing. Empty benches, a lady with two children giving her a wide berth as they enter the building, and no madwoman running away.

✳

That night, the steel-trap mouth of teeth from her childhood terrors drops from a stifling, close sky. She screams through a thousand heavy veils of sleep. She fights to wrest her shoulders from gravity's sharp claws holding her to the bed. The mouth, made of brushed steel plates bolted

(142)

together with mismatched shards of glass, pauses, assesses its prey. The monster grows, from room-sized to apartment-sized, bigger. Tia sends as much energy as she can muster through every muscle. If the thing had a tongue, it would lick the incisor closest to her, an X-acto knife the size of a plane's propeller. Her body does not respond.

Death. This is what death feels like.

The light changes, softening, and the mouth shrinks, floats back. Tia's eyelids are the first to respond. She blinks. The mouth trap disappears. In its place, Andrew looks almost as afraid as she feels, his hands tight around her shoulders. The scream has come out. She can hear it now. She shuts her mouth. Andrew's weight bears down on her, his thumbs digging into her coracoid process. It fucking hurts.

'I've never seen a night terror before,' Andrew says softly, a person rapt at the scene of an accident.

The next night, the mouth trap takes a different tack and appears from under the bed. When Tia comes to in the lamp-lit bedroom, the sheets stick to her skin. Her first instinct is to check if she peed. It's sweat. Much of Andrew's concern has been replaced by irritation.

'Banshee,' he says. 'I think that is the word for screaming like that.'

Tia takes the couch on night number three, and the steel mouth leaves her alone. On the fourth night, back in bed, it reappears. Tia comes to in the dark, alone. She struggles for purchase, lands on the light under the bathroom door. By the time Andrew returns to bed, Tia has changed her pyjamas and the sheets.

They sit with the light on. Stare into the space at the end of their bed. Adrenaline gives Tia the sense she's floating just above the mattress.

'I don't know what this is,' Andrew says, with no attempt to filter the honesty, 'but it needs to stop.'

Tia spends the rest of the night on the couch. In the restless sleep that takes her from the small hours to pre-dawn, she remembers instructions she once received, as a child. 'You are being held down and you can't fight back. Do not fight back. You are not alone. You are in SP. Scrunch up your face.' SP. Sleep paralysis.

As soon as she wakes, she's on her computer, looking him up, Ira the sleep specialist. Is both surprised and relieved to see he still has a practice. She calls right away, speaking quietly into the phone, leaving a message. The sun hasn't yet risen.

Andrew enters the room, the wrecked shuffle of a man who didn't sleep when he needed to. Guilt jabs her in the stomach.

You should leave him. You know he would be better off without you.

Tears sting her eyes. What kind of thought is that?

No.

'Who was that?' Andrew asks.

'Oh, no one. Checking my voice mail.' Slippery like a candy, the lie.

'You were talking.'

'Oh yeah, probably,' she says, even though she knows Andrew hates hearing *you might be right*. When Andrew states something, it becomes fact. 'It was a client. They called in the middle of the night.' The slippery candy tastes sour. *Can't take it back now.*

Andrew yawns, throat clucking, and then sighs. 'Well, thank goodness you had your ringer off.' He disappears into the bedroom. A couple of moments later the shower rushes on.

Tia slumps into the couch. Lets her old friend anxiety rush from her in tears and doesn't fight the chest-shuddering sobs. She sits there and takes it, watching the sun slowly light their living room. By the time Andrew's shower stops, so have her tears.

She's pouring boiling water onto freshly ground beans when Andrew steals up behind her, wraps his arms around her waist. She puts the kettle on the counter, lets her head fall against his deltoid.

'Bacon and eggs?' he says.

'With tomatoes, from the garden,' she answers. She raises her head. 'No toast, though. We're out of bread.'

'I'll get some.'

'Oh no, I don't need any, it's fine.' Tia twists in his arms, looks over her shoulder at his chin, his cheekbone. Her eyeballs ache with the strain.

'I want some. I'll get it. Five minutes.' He releases her as quickly as he snatched her. She stares at her hand on the white plastic kettle, the half-filled carafe of leaching coffee grounds. It's not until the door closes behind Andrew that she remembers what she was doing.

Chapter 23

Holy fucking shit, it was Pacifique.

On the phone, with Tia.

And now she's here, at the fucking supermarket.

The woman in line for the till vibrates like one of those holographic images from *Star Trek*, in part brighter than her surroundings, in part hazier.

Cunt, Andrew hisses.

A bald man wearing a Harley-Davidson T-shirt and examining cereal boxes at the end of an aisle stiffens and gives him a look. Andrew sucks in his bottom lip. He did not mean to say that out loud.

Idiot, he thinks, mouth firmly shut.

He breaks stride, avoids the man, arcs out of his way. This allows him a half-panoramic view of the woman. The woman of his girlfriend's dreams. She cannot be more than five feet tall, but her spine reaches heavenward like a skyscraper. Posture like a ballerina. Her black hair is divided into two ponytails – *pigtails*, he reminds himself – and one disappears out of sight over a shoulder. The other lies against her right shoulder blade, hangs halfway down her back. The part is perfectly straight, in line with that perfect spine, and shoots north and south white like a snowdrift. *White?* Her ears, the backs of her bare arms, the long, muscled legs in shorts like Tia wears, except not nearly as well as this woman, they are all brown. Just her scalp, white against the black curling hair. The woman weaves slightly from side to side to a song only she can hear. She wears a faded black jean jacket once sporting arms, now frayed at the shoulders. It ends several inches above her hips and so, too, does the black shirt she wears underneath. Her lower back tight and muscled like those legs. Black short shorts hug her ass and he does not see a single panty line. The same drum thrums in his gut, and this time his cock responds on the off-beat. *Fucking hell.* He turns away, considers cereal, the price of gas, which he doesn't know, what Dr. Benson will think when he tells her this. His chub shrivels. Dr. Benson. Pacifique.

Pacifique?

What in Christ's name is she doing here?

This, this, this – don't make sense.

He runs his tongue once, twice, three times over dry lips, chews off a bit of chap.

That cunt, Pacifique, here in town and stringing Tia along this whole fucking time.

Andrew swivels again, one step and then another, he's not sure what he'll do but he really must sort this out and this woman has *got, got, she's got to fucking understand* what she's done to Tia, what she's done to them, *to me.* Pacifique turns then, as if she's heard him, and she faces him straight-on and boy is she not as beautiful as Tia made her out to be, pretty painted on with too much makeup. That pigtail flowing over her chest is a kinky wave, not the ringlets of Tia's stories, and more mahogany in colour, certainly not black. He catches her eye and then loses it as she scans something behind him.

She's looking for someone.

For Tia?

She sticks a long fingernail in her mouth, and now he's only a few feet from her, at the back of the queue, and he's caught her eye again and *she's giving me a face*, like the face the bald guy gave. Her tan darkens in the lines at the corners of her mouth.

Things aren't what they seem, mate.

'Excuse me, sorry,' he says, with as much sanity as he can muster, and does not even allow himself to touch the woman as he goes by. To touch her would only serve to remind him of his terrible mistake, remind him how much his pride has cost him. He will not tell Dr. Benson about this.

He nearly knocks the automatic door with his forehead on his way into the parking lot, everything going too slow and him going too fast.

How to tell Dr. Benson he is seeing things again? And seeing not his visions, but Tia's?

Chapter 24

Andrew bursts into the apartment. Splotches mark his cheeks, the rest of his face canvas-white.

'That was – '

The front door swings wide and hits the wall behind it, cutting her off. She grasps the arm of the couch. With the other hand, she recalibrates her grip on the coffee mug.

'An – '

'I saw your fucking girlfriend,' he interrupts in a single, hyperventilated breath, staring at the area rug that separates them.

'My – '

'At least, I thought I did.' He looks at her and laughs, an ear-piercing, hysterical giggling that makes Tia flinch. He doesn't stop.

No sudden movements flashes through her head. She leans forward, places the mug on the hardwood at her feet. Tucks it close to the bottom of the couch.

'Andrew?' she attempts when the man, on the verge of another fainting spell, pauses for a quarter-breath. 'What's wrong?'

His laughter cuts off with one final shriek as he collapses to the floor. He's on his ass before Tia can make it to him. Not unconscious. Tia crouches close to his listing side. He stares into a distance she cannot fathom, a point between them and the couch, a spot where a reality only he can see shimmers with possibility and subterfuge.

'Andrew, sweetie. Please tell me.' *No more hiding.*

'I thought I did. I thought I saw her.'

'Who, sweetie? Who did you see?' Was this what his parents endured? Is this what she has to look forward to?

'Your girlfriend,' he says, voice heavy. His breathing returns to a rhythm approaching normal. A vibration like fever chills runs through him. His knees knock.

Tia counts the heartbeats that hammer under her palm, which cups his left scapula. 'Honey, you're my boyfriend. Do you mean boyfriend?'

'Pacifique!'

Tia wobbles. Her left hand shoots back, catching her, and the wrist sings with the impact.

He said that. He said it when he came in. 'I saw your fucking girlfriend.' Who else could he have meant?

'That doesn't make sense.' Tia scours her brain for the day's schedule and cannot find it. Could she sleep today? Sleep for days. She would like that.

'That's what I said,' Andrew says in a steady voice. He notices her then. 'I'm sorry. I didn't see her. I thought I did.'

Panic sprouts in three places at once: the back of Tia's throat, somewhere under her heart's right atrium, and in her abdomen, transverse abdominis gripping her large intestine like angry fists. Her heart rate shoots from normal to arrhythmic. 'You're upset. You were so upset. Why say you saw her if you didn't?' The words rush together, and she wishes she could help it but she can't. 'I don't understand.'

Andrew shifts, makes to come closer, and she scoots away on the slick wood floor.

'No. No.'

'I'm sorry,' he says again. 'Christ, Tia, I'm sorry. She looked so much like Pacifique, you have no idea.'

'And how the fuck would you know what she looks like, you arrogant prick?' The words escape like bullets. The kick back hits her in the stomach.

Andrew collapses against the door, face slack.

'I'm sorry. I'm sorry.' She reaches for him, and now he's the one shrinking away. 'Andrew. I didn't mean it. I swear.'

'Yes, you did,' he says with a strange, slight smile. 'That's okay. It's true.'

Tia shakes her head. She cannot bring the words *It's not* to her lips. Andrew doesn't expect her to. Is this the moment it all ends? Isn't that the sort of thing you only see in retrospect? This is more likely her giving up, like she is wont to do. Everything in her life has always taken her so much longer than she thought it ought to. And, often, things left unfinished. Her mother used the word *lazy* a lot when she was young. It wasn't laziness.

She finds herself leaning against the door beside Andrew. Their arms don't touch. Their breaths come long and deep. In tandem. A cycle of carbon dioxide from one to the other. Tia searches for the spot in the middle of their living room, the one Andrew glommed onto when he came in shouting of an imaginary woman. If she could find the spot. No. There is nothing here but the spare living room of two people who don't care much about decorating, who don't have much money. The sun has climbed a few degrees. The area rug lies half in blazing morning light. Their feet stretch in front of them. Andrew has his boots on. His workboots. She is about to say something and then decides not to. Instead, she lets gravity, the pull of him, her lover, her best friend, guide her head to his shoulder. There is no flinch, no pullback. His head falls onto hers. Who cries first? She cannot tell. One of his tears hits her left temple. It runs into her eye, stings. She blinks it away, and with it comes her own.

'Oh, Andrew,' she says, and pushes through all the resistance in her own body, the resistance she expects in his, and turns to him, runs her arms around his neck.

'I am so sorry,' he says.

She doesn't know what he means this time.

Andrew returns the hug with a hug of his own. When he pulls his head back, it's not to disengage. He presses damp lips to Tia's, then pushes, harder, his familiar tongue a gift to her. She twists her spine to get a better angle, to better accept his kiss. They rush into each other, Andrew's hair in her fingers. He grasps her neck in his wide palm. They collapse to the floor, Tia's elbow hitting the hardwood with a knock.

Nothing interrupts them. Tia unlaces one of Andrew's boots while he removes the other. Her pyjamas slip off. Without speaking, they move to the area rug, its scratch somehow more civilized than the hard, dusty floor. When Andrew cups his hand over Tia's mons pubis and presses a finger inside her, finds the river there, he gasps. Tia hears her own wetness, imagines it dripping to the rug below. Andrew's cock digs into her thigh, pulses with a fresh surge of blood. She pulls his hand from her cunt, pulls until his hand is at her face. She opens her mouth and he places one and then both fingers in. She closes her teeth softly around the first knuckles, tasting herself. She doesn't let go of his fingers when she scoots out from under him. He rolls onto his back. She straddles him, reaches between her legs, finds his penis, and, without a word, fanfare, pause, sits down. The welcome discomfort makes her groan. Andrew grunts under her, clasping her bottom teeth with his fingers. His thumb cradles her chin. He pulls. She falls to him, breasts meeting his soft chest, mouth and teeth searching for his lips. When they kiss, it's two lips and Andrew's fingers. Finally, he pulls the fingers out, Tia's teeth scraping the skin. He clutches the back of Tia's head, pulls her hard to him. Their teeth crack together. Tia bucks her hips in a rhythmic wave. She tries to pull back, make room to touch herself. Andrew won't release his grip. He sucks in his stomach and she snakes a hand between them, finds her slippery clitoris. The orgasm a button waiting to be pushed. She moans into Andrew's mouth, and he replies with a swifter tempo in his hips. His hold on her neck loosens.

'Wait, are you going to come?' she asks.

'I think I might,' he says.

How? she wonders. The man never comes. The meds have made it all but impossible.

'Come then,' she says.

He clamps his eyes shut and opens his mouth, releasing Tia's lip. She slips her right hand from his crown to the back of his skull, pulls.

'Look at me and come,' she says, the climax slithering up her thighs.

Andrew's eyes snap open and he looks, the muscles in his jaw clenched like every muscle in Tia's pelvis. When they come, his focus falters, and she says, again: 'Look at me.'

He does.

＊

'You'll need to see Benson,' she says.

They've been lying for some indeterminate amount of time, the sun slowly baking the sweat off their skin. Tia slept briefly. It has been weeks since she felt so relaxed. As the glow dissipates, the words from earlier peek through the foggy sex-brain like rust coming through a hasty paint job.

'About seeing ... things.'

Andrew should be defensive. She has not chosen her words carefully. He's not. He remains calm and still beside her. 'I know,' is all he says.

A line crossed. A spectrum travelled. None of this madness as straight-forward as any of the analogies used. Tia lets another couple of minutes tick by and then unhooks her arm from Andrew's. He doesn't resist. He doesn't move. She sits. Andrew's come dribbles out of her and she palms what she can. Her knees crack as she struggles to her feet.

Andrew studies her, her face, for an instant, then the parts of her only he gets to see: what her mother calls 'child-bearing hips,' wide and covered with a soft coat of fat, puberty's stretch marks an alien purple flowing under the surface like subterranean rivers; breasts as big as Andrew's palms, and small and high enough to let loose in T-shirts on days off, or, in her younger years, to barely conceal under a sequin-studded tank top at the bar; alabaster upper thighs lightly dusted with golden brown pubic hair.

'You really are beautiful,' he says.

Tia glances at his cock lying flaccid, unaffected, on his thigh.

The compliment does what compliments are meant to do: the rush of warmth in her abdomen, a tiny hint of a blush, a sort of caving in on herself, a self-consciousness. 'Thank you.'

She lets him admire her, this body she has lived with for twenty-four years, before heading to the bathroom. Lets her hips sway. When she gets to the bedroom door she pauses, grabs the door frame, juts one hip out, hikes a leg, props it against the frame. She looks over her shoulder and grins at Andrew, who doesn't laugh exactly, but he smiles, and it's enough.

※

Andrew has put on pyjamas and sits at his computer. He won't dress until he's showered. He is squeamish about the particular brand of filth that comes with fucking.

Tia shoves her feet into sneakers at the front door. 'I'll get toast. Bread. I think we need to eat.'

Andrew swivels. 'She's not there. She's not going to be there.'

'I know, Andrew.' She does, she does know. 'I really just want toast. Honestly. Do you want to come with me? I'll wait for you.'

'No.' Without hesitation.

'I can go?'

He thinks about this. Does he understand what she just did, handing over her agency like that? Or does he understand that, in fact, she said those exact words so she could maintain it? 'Of course. I would like toast, too. And peanut butter.'

'We have some,' she says by reflex. 'I'll get more. Then we're all stocked.' Is this how housewives and businessmen of the sixties spoke to each other? It's not so hard. She turns before he can say anything more, before she can see anything more, know anything more. Mentally exit like she used to do in hospital with O'Shea.

※

Tia buys bread at the customer service counter. Fewer people, less eye contact to avoid. She pockets the change, tucks the loaf under her arm, and her phone rings. She drops the bread on the grocery store linoleum, scrabbles for it, tucks it under the right arm, snags the phone from her back pocket, and catches the call before it goes to voice mail.

'This is Janey at Dr. Eckstein's office returning your call,' says the voice on the other end. Janey, Ira's assistant and his wife. Tia forgot that detail until this moment. Janey sounds the same, sweet and calm, a slowness to her words befitting someone who teaches English as a second language. Or someone who deals daily with people on the edge.

'Oh. Yes.' She avoids a parking-lot puddle by a centimetre. It must have rained last night.

'When would you like to come in?'

'I don't know.' Tia left her daytimer at home. Janey doesn't say anything. The silence spreads out two seconds, then several. 'Let me think.'

'Of course, Tia,' says Janey.

Tia slows to a stop in an empty parking space. 'I remember you,' she says.

'And I remember you,' Janey says.

'Oh, I doubt that.' Not even a pen in her pocket to write down the appointment.

'It's true. You spent a lot of time here. We had some nice conversations. You probably don't recall.'

Tia doesn't. Recalls Janey's face, heart-shaped and high-cheekboned, her thick and expertly plucked brows. How right they looked on Janey's face, so unlike Tia's mother's thin brows, tweezed to oblivion and filled in with a pencil that was not quite the right shade of brown. In Tia's memory, Janey's lips don't move. No conversations.

'When is Ira free next?' Tia finally says.

'If it's urgent, Tia, we can fit you in soon. You tell me what works for you.'

Tia drops to a seat on a stall curb. 'I don't know. I'm sorry.' Something twinges in her low back.

'What about Monday, Tia? At noon?'

Her schedule finally appears in front of her – class, clients, the same old thing. Why was it so hard for her to tell Janey when she was free? 'Yes. Yes, I can make that work.'

She hangs up, pushes to her feet, the out-of-alignment vertebra humming in her lumbar spine, and returns the phone to her pocket. She steps over the concrete parking block, then stops, fishes out the phone. She deletes the calls to and from Ira's office. Checks the history, yes, they're gone. There's no call to her voice mail in the history either, which will give her away if Andrew goes snooping. If she calls her voice mail now, it won't make sense, the time stamp will be off. But not calling her voice mail is better than calling Ira. She'll tell Andrew, she will, once she's sure. Right now she's not even sure if this is right, if she should be talking to anyone about anything. Will it go on record? Will someone call and say, 'We hear you're crazy again. You know what this means, right?'

Tia shakes the paranoia from her head, which has in typical fashion spiralled into her gut. Food will fix that. She tucks the bread tight to her rib cage. Forgetting all of this will fix that. Forget everything except Monday at noon. Monday at noon.

Chapter 25

'Beatrice?'

'It's Bernice, dear. Dr. Benson's running about ten minutes behind today, so just take a seat.' Beatrice nods to the chairs on the opposite side of the waiting room and returns her attention to the computer screen.

Andrew follows her nod and sees, yes, the same office chairs Benson had last week and the week before that and, as far as he can remember, last year. Why is Beatrice working for Dr. Benson? Why does she not remember him?

'Oh, I apologize for the state of the magazines,' she says. 'All the good ones go missing and I haven't restocked. No *Adbusters*, no *Wired*. *Psychology Today*?'

Beatrice must have taken a medical office assistant course, like they advertise on the bus. Gotten her mole removed.

Nope, not Beatrice.

Bernice. Fuck.

Bernice is trying to make a joke, waiting.

'Oh! Yes, very funny, Bernice,' he says, as if nothing at all is the matter. 'You know *Psychology Today* is all pap.'

Bernice laughs the way she always laughs, which is sweetly and kindly and innocently. He knows she is not innocent. The things she must have seen working for Benson.

Beatrice, Bernice, old fat ladies the both of them. One of them real, one of them fantasy.

Andrew takes a chair. Counts each finger, his two thumbs. He tied his laces, he zipped his fly. He runs a hand over the front of his shirt: no dried-on food. No stains in the hand-wiping zone on the thighs of his blue jeans. Does not risk looking. Instead pictures himself taking the shirt, clean from the closet, earlier that morning. He looks fine. He is fine.

There are lines and he can see them and if he takes care he will colour inside them and no one will be the wiser, not even himself.

Ten minutes becomes twenty. Andrew zones out on a *Vanity Fair* photo spread of extraterrestrial women on the surface of what might be Mars. He thinks they might be mixing up their planets and he hopes the photographer knew that. No Martian would ever model for *Vanity Fair*. One woman reminds him of an Amazonian anorexic version of Tia. She has white-blond hair, blown out with some kind of hair product or maybe a fan like they use in photo shoots, and she's standing on what could be a mountain or a molehill, depending on perspective. The hill appears to be made of red moon dust and Andrew spends several minutes trying to decide if the model is meant to look taller than a mountain or simply standard explorer-sized (if explorers of the Old World had been women, over six feet tall, and 110 pounds). He decides it is unclear, that the photographer did not decide. They have done up the model in white pancake makeup and drawn shadows under her eyes, which makes a woman who might be pretty look ugly; he supposes this was also intended. The woman's gaze verges on empty. Underneath, though, he can see something, the 'motivation,' and he remembers Tia turning in her wheelchair at the nurses' station that first night, her expression wild and desperate and very much insane. Afraid. The woman crushing mountains on the bizarre Moon-Mars appears confident and strong. Underneath it all, though: fear.

He watches the feet of a patient leave and he closes the magazine. Sits and quiets his mind while he waits for Benson to call him in. When she does, he smiles, rises, and follows her into the office, closing the door behind him.

'What's going on, Andrew?' Benson says before she even takes the chair beside her desk.

May I be Frank? idles through his thoughts.

'I do not quite know.' There is my girlfriend, for one. And *her* girl-friend. *Ex.* Who knows? Andrew perches on the edge of a chair, back straight, hands carefully unknotted in his lap. He swallows. 'I know I am not feeling ... right.'

'Okay. Let's deal with that.'

Why did he think he had to worry about this appointment? Benson does not care about the system and where they fit in. She cares only for his well-being.

'Tell me about this not feeling right.'

He tells her. Provides a careful summary of the past week – minus Pacifique and the fight, and sex, with Tia. They go back and forth, and his posture softens a little like it can when he actually relaxes. They talk like they have many times before. It is easy.

She's a bloody doctor, let her do the work.

'Your nanny, Beatrice?'

Good work, mate.

Why did he say that? 'For a millisecond. Less. I have never before noticed, but Bernice has similar looks to Beatrice – how I imagined Beatrice to look. It is really just that for comfort, as a young child, I chose a grandmotherly, kindly old lady. Not that Bernice is old. Well, you know what I mean.'

This is where Benson is supposed to say she does or does not know what he means. Instead, she says nothing. She does not write anything down either. Andrew does not trust himself to say anything else, so he waits her out.

'Have you seen anyone else?' she asks. She jots on the pad in her lap.

Why, Dr. Benson, whatever do you mean?

She looks up. 'Have you seen other people from your imaginary life in your real life?'

'No,' he says with a shake of his head. He gazes off to one side, think-ing. He thinks only of Pacifique, but he works his brain around in case he can fool Benson. 'Just Beatrice slash Bernice. Kinda dumb, eh?' He attempts a smile he hopes appears sheepish.

Benson studies him. 'It's not dumb, Andrew. I think it's something we need to pay attention to. You know as well as I do that your disease can get out of control very quickly.'

'Yeah, you're right.' He imagines the defunct blue bridge between Victoria and Esquimalt, the span cantilevered open for water traffic. The steel deck below. He clenches his buttocks. *Shut. It.* 'I'm not sleeping well. What do you think? Do we need to look at my meds? Could they be … ?'

'We certainly can. Our bodies and our brains are not static things. Their response to drugs, to life' – she says this with a rise in her voice, as if she too might have a life outside of these walls, which Andrew has tried and always failed to imagine – 'changes. So, let's see if we can get you some better sleep and get you feeling less scattered. And for a little bit, anyway, let's continue seeing each other more often.'

He sighs with relief. Benson's face warms for the first time, and they start talking medications and dosages and sleep schedules and how is school going, anyway, does he still feel interested in the material, and he does not say anything more that means anything at all.

He did not lie, he tells himself in the elevator, a prescription and a card reminding him of his next appointment folded into his pocket. Benson asked if he had seen anyone else from his imaginary life in the real world. He had not. Pacifique is not of his imaginary world.

He passes the supermarket where he may have seen Pacifique, which houses the pharmacy. He pauses at the spot where sidewalk meets parking lot. Then he continues home. There are things that he must do.

Chapter 26

She fails to tell Andrew about Ira, and each day it becomes more difficult to come clean. *Why did you lie?* he will ask, and she will have to admit she doesn't know. She will have to admit there are things she doesn't want him to know and she isn't sure why.

Ira works in a different building now, a swankier place downtown that has a *This building is a historic site* plaque next to the main doors. He's four floors up, and through a crack between buildings, she sees the harbour shimmering like liquid stars in late summer heat.

The lines that fracture Ira's temples and cheeks run deep. Still, he doesn't look sixteen years older. He must be almost sixty. He looks great, different. Handsome even.

'Wow, Tia,' he says, leaning forward. The leather desk chair is also swankier, ergonomic, accessorized with a motley crew of handles and levers. 'I can't get over it. I would have recognized you anywhere.'

'I still look eight?'

'In a way, yes.' He smiles and his lips break over straight white teeth. 'I also can't get over seeing you again. I guess it means things are not going so well, but I can't deny I'm happy to see you.'

His face is different, his mouth. Tia remembers. She breathes in through her nose. No halitosis. She brings a hand to her face, gestures at her own mouth, and Ira laughs.

'It really has been a while, hasn't it? Years ago I got a whole bunch of work done. Even had my jaw broken and wired shut.'

She cringes.

'Got a great mouth of teeth now. I look a bit changed.' He glows with happiness. He closes his mouth, and the light in his face dims.

'How are you, Tia?'

She wants to say, *Fine*. No, she wants to say, *Good*. Tears fill her lower lids. Her ears flare hot. The office disappears in a buzz and all she sees is Ira's expression, dusted with compassion and something else. *Where have you been, Ira?* She manages a shrug.

Ira fills the silence. 'I'm still doing sleep stuff, with my clients. Other things, too. Treating adults, for one, doing hypnotherapy.'

'Hypnosis?'

'It's really interesting. I've had clients make tremendous break-throughs using hypnosis.'

'I sleep pretty well now,' Tia says to the floor. Except for the past week.

'I'm glad to hear that.'

Ira watches her. She scans for something else to look at. A degree on the wall. *College of Physicians and Surgeons of the Province of British Columbia, the degree of medical doctor. Joseph Earl Eckstein.*

'Since when are you a doctor? A real doctor. I mean – '

'I've been a medical doctor since the seventies, Tia.' Ira smiles, not offended.

Who told Tia he was *just* a PhD? Her mother? Her mother. Tia shakes her head.

Then Ira winks, and Tia remembers being six.

'Next time T. Rex comes,' Ira said, 'think of me.' Ira worked exclusively with children then, so his office looked like other child-friendly places – pediatric hospitals, daycares, the kids' corner at her mother's doctor's office – with its board books, the roller coaster of wooden beads on wire loop-de-loops, a well-loved Cabbage Patch Kid named Stan, a child-sized plastic table and chairs permanently embossed with crayons. They sat wherever Tia wanted to, and that day she chose a beanbag chair. Ira had one big enough for him, in faded brown. Tia picked the small pink one. It felt safe and tasted like strawberry. Flavour transferred through her seat, up her spine, and into her mouth. She had told Ira this at an earlier appointment and then clamped her hand over her mouth. Ira had said, 'I wish my chair tasted like strawberry.' They'd both looked at his brown chair and thought the same grody thought and Tia had giggled herself right onto the Milky Way–inspired carpet.

'Think of you?' Tia garbled over the two fingers she had jammed in her mouth.

'Yes, me. I'm kind of like T. Rex. I'm big and tall and I have these funny little arms – ' he tucked his elbows and waggled his claw-fingers and she laughed, releasing the fingertips from her mouth ' – and these horrible teeeeth!' At this he shouted and opened that awful, putrid maw, and his teeth were like knives falling from his mottled gums. Tia shrieked, not entirely in delight, and lost her balance on the beanbag. When she righted herself, she stole a glance at Ira. He placidly returned her gaze, mouth safely closed, and then winked.

When T. Rex came back, it roared as it always did through the door of her bedroom, somehow not having to duck, terrorizing and barely six feet tall at the same time, and she screamed as hard as she could, except she screamed only in her head. She remembered the words: 'You are in SP. Scrunch up your face.' She did. The monster paused, mouth gaping, ready to bend and tear her flesh from her perfect, delicious bones. Then it winked.

She laughed. For a moment, the dinosaur laughed with her, laughed in a way only Tyrannosaurus Rexes can, its tiny arms waving in tiny circles. Then the creature disappeared. Popped like a balloon. Tia turned over, stuck her fingers in her mouth, and fell asleep.

She'd forgotten about T. Rex.

'I can't get over how good a job they did on your teeth,' she says, and then shrivels. 'I'm sorry. God, I don't know what's wrong with me.'

'Relax, Tia. We're old friends. And you're right. Magic, this.' Ira digs into his jaw with square-tipped fingers. 'It was a little girl who told me how bad things were. I mean, I knew, but she put it out there.'

Me? she wonders.

'Not you. You noticed, obviously. I think it made an impression on a lot of people. You don't think about these things. It's quality of life, your teeth, your breath. Sometimes you need someone totally unexpected to tell you the obvious.'

'I used to call you Ira.'

'From *Where the Wild Things Are*.'

'Yes!'

'You told me. I remember. Do I still look like Ira?'

'Not anymore. But it's been your name in my head for so long – '

'Use it. My first name is Joseph. You can use Ira if it helps. Or Joseph. Whatever you like.'

Tia sits in a giant leather chair, big enough for someone twice her size. She scoots her butt out a couple of inches and hikes one knee and then the other under her chin. She sticks her middle finger into her mouth and chews the rough nail there. The seat wraps around her like a hug. She finds the sparkling slip of harbour through the buildings.

'Where are you?' Ira's voice sounds the same as it did when she was a little girl.

'On the sea. In a boat.'

'A rowboat?'

Tia settles deeper into the chair and adjusts the cushion at her lower back. She sighs. 'Hmm, no. Not a big boat, but bigger than a rowboat. One with sails. Oars, too, if you want them. I don't know much about boats.'

'Sounds like a sailboat. A small one.'

'But not too small. It has to be safe.'

'Of course. With life jackets.'

'I always wear a life jacket. My dad taught me that.'

'He taught you well.'

The brain is a computer, she once read. Microprocessors constantly working. And not working. She's built of many not-working microprocessors, she decides. She clears her throat and leaves the harbour behind. Ira holds eye contact, his face open, calm.

'What am I doing here?' She is not open or calm. She is glitchy.

The counsellor's calmness stirs into a slight smile. 'Usually you tell me that.'

She laughs mildly. A frog waits quiet behind her vocal cords. 'I guess I'm upset.' It comes out easily. 'A lot has gone on since … since a long time.'

Ira sits forward in his chair, feet flat on the floor. He bends at the waist, slouching slightly, and clasps his hands in the space between his knees. He looks like he could stay this way forever. At least an hour. Which, Tia supposes, must be the point.

'It would take forever to tell you everything that has happened,' she offers finally, with a shake of her head. 'I – ' The frog ribbits. She grimaces and holds out both hands, palms up.

'I don't need your full history. We don't have to go there. We can imagine we've had one or two of those kinds of meetings, you've caught me up on everything, and today we're talking. Talking about how you feel today. Nothing from the past.'

'It's fucked up, Ira,' she says, and that's when the crying starts. No warning, just tears. A whole bucketful down her face and onto her bare knees. 'Shit, sorry.' She reaches for the tissues at the same moment Ira hands the box to her and she scrabbles for several. She presses them to her face, and they are quickly soaked. She gets more.

Ira lets her cry. A good two minutes pass before she sighs some sense into herself.

He says, 'I believe you. I do. I won't say I've seen it all because I haven't. I have seen some seriously fucked-up shit, though' – Tia can't help a smile – 'and I'll see a lot more before I leave this place. Your fucked-up shit is among friends here.'

He does a strange thing. Not strange, no: unexpected. He opens the hands clasped until then between his knees and offers them to Tia. She doesn't hesitate, she takes them, and calm rushes into her. She sniffs hard, catches some fresh snot and half-grins, half-grimaces.

'Okay. I'll do it.' A pause and then: 'Whatever *it* is.'

'Good!' He releases her hands, straightens his spine, and, voice clear and driven like a coach in the locker room, says, 'Let's get to work.'

'Work' turns out to be more chit-chat, and Tia wonders if Ira has created the best racket ever: charge yuppies more than a hundred bucks an hour to socialize. Tia tells him about the things that don't involve being in love with an imaginary woman. She tells him about getting a biology degree, then deciding she couldn't sit in a lab for the rest of her life, which is how she got into massage therapy. She tells him she is living with a man named Andrew who is training to be a journeyman electrician, and they love each other. She says her mom is the same and her dad seems okay. She mentions only two ugly things: the night terrors and that a bicycle accident caused brain injury–induced psychosis, that she was institutionalized for two months. She does not provide details. Does not mention Pacifique.

With a few minutes left, Ira mentions hypnotherapy again. 'I think it will help you.'

'With the dreams?'

'Hypnotherapy is helpful for so many things – trauma, addiction, anxiety, depression, repressed memories, sleep issues, you name it.'

'Repressed memories? Isn't that a bit woo-woo?'

'No, not at all. It's basic science. We don't remember everything that happens to us. Not always because of repression, but sometimes.'

'As far as I understand, people repress stuff for good reason,' says Tia.

'Yes, often for good reason. Again, though, not always. And what's good at one point in a person's life might not be good for them later on.'

'I'm not sure I understand.'

'It's not something I can explain in five minutes. It's not something I want to rush you into either. I won't ask you to do anything you're not comfortable with.'

She smiles her thanks.

'Are you interested?' he asks.

'Of course. Who wouldn't be?'

He nods. 'It is fascinating. I'm continually blown away by the effect it has on people. Okay, let's do this: we'll meet in about a week and talk about it some more.'

'That's it. That's my homework? No T. Rex to-do list?'

It takes him a moment. The memory crawls through years of viscera, and Ira breaks into his big, toothy smile. 'No T. Rex to-do list. I'll see you next week. We've got all the time in the world.'

What an odd thing to say, especially for someone who must have seen a lot of the opposite in his life. It sounds sweet and makes her think, for a split second, that it's true.

As soon as she gets home, her mother calls.

'Do you have secateurs?' Yvonne asks.

Tia hears water and clinking in the background, her mother doing dishes. 'Sectors?'

'No, secateurs,' her mother says again, slowly and overloud. 'For gardening.'

Tia can't even picture the word in her head. 'I don't know what you're talking about, Mom.' Why would her mom think she has such a tool, given she just started half-heartedly gardening this summer? 'Ask Shirley.'

Yvonne huffs. She and Shirley will never be friends.

'Oh,' says Tia, 'guess who I ran into the other day? I – Joseph Eckstein, the sleep specialist.' It slips out.

'Jo Eckstein! Well. What is he doing these days?'

Jo. Tia feels a familiar annoyance bubble in her stomach. Why does this of all things interest her mother so much?

'Oh, the same, I think. Still doing counselling, with adults now, too. And hypnotherapy. Which, I don't know … ' She didn't mean to mention the hypnosis either. She wants this conversation to be over.

'Huh. Like past lives?'

Tia shrugs into the phone and then remembers her mother can't see her. 'I have no idea, Mom. I think it's supposed to be a bit more … medical than that.'

'Hypnosis is hardly medical. It's weird. And fascinating. I read this book in university, *Sybil*. It's all about this woman with split personality and her therapist using hypnosis to identify all her selves. Strangest stuff I ever read, I tell you.'

Ira described hypnosis as 'fascinating,' too. 'I've told you, Mom, it's dissociative identity disorder. Most people with DID do not appreciate being called "split personality."'

Her mother enjoys forgetting her daughter ever spent time in the loony bin. Or that she is shacked up with Andrew, who has told her about numerous times he's encountered otherwise intelligent people who think he's some nutcase with a hundred people living in his head.

'I know, I know, but that's what we called it then.' Tia's mother sighs on the other end of the line, not at all upset. Pleased. 'I haven't thought about that book in years. Well, if you see Jo again, tell him Yvonne says hi.'

Flirting. That's the excitement in her mother's voice. Tia shudders. *How tacky.* Tia hangs up and goes straight to Andrew's computer. *Sybil,* from the looks of Wikipedia, is complete bollocks, as Andrew might say. She clicks page after page that talks about hypnosis and how it can be used as a treatment for pretty much everything. Nowhere does she find evidence that it can be used for repressed memories. People write about being tricked by their therapists into remembering something that could not be true. Ira wouldn't trick her. At least, she doesn't think so. The further she investigates, the more she thinks Ira might have gotten into the pseudo-science her mother accused him of practising almost twenty years ago. Tia was on his side then. Has he changed? Or is it she who has changed, her adult mind closed, unwilling? *What would Pacifique do?*

The thought comes unbidden. With it the usual cramping, the heart race. *Oh, fuck it:* what would Pacifique do? Pacifique would jump in, that's what she would do. And she would tell Tia to jump in, too.

Chapter 27

Andrew believes in intuition. Intuition is a map to a place no one has ever been. The maddest of the mad have always exhibited this gift. Along with the brightest of the bright, the bravest of the brave. He has never considered himself the bravest or the brightest or the maddest, even when he was his maddest, his brightest, but he knows that when he is lucky, intuition smiles on him. It is magic. For this reason, Andrew does not discount the realization he had last week, the morning Tia lied about the phone call. He knew then and he knows now that someone else is in her life. Intuition goes only so far: it will not tell him who. First he thought it was Pacifique. That was likely a vision. Possibly. Uncertain, in any case. It requires further investigation, which he will do. Besides the fact Pacifique is a figment of Tia's (and now his) imagination, Tia's daytimer tells a different story about whom she is seeing. Someone named Ira. A man. At least, Andrew is pretty sure Ira is a man's name. The name has a faint touch of familiarity. These days, everything is familiar. He cannot recall Tia mentioning it. Perhaps he is a new person in her life. Where would she have met him? Would she not have mentioned him in passing at some point? Andrew does not know. His memory flows and then clots.

Let it sit, mate, you'll figure it out.

It occurs to him, because Tia writes *Ira: 11:00* in her book, that Ira could be someone who is not a date. He could be a dentist, her chiropractor, the dog groomer. Tia has never referred to her dentist by his first name. Andrew checks, anyway. He does not remember the name of Tia's chiropractor but he remembers where that person works, remembers the chiropractor is a woman. The man who works in the same office is not an Ira. And Tia does not have a dog. Although Tia has said several times recently she wants one. Maybe she has been going to meet with a dog breeder behind his back? Where would she get the money for a purebred dog? Maybe she found an ad online. Of all the things to lie about.

No. A thorough Internet search results in nothing. There is no professional in town named Ira providing any kind of service Tia may require. Ira is either a man she has to make scheduled appointments with to have this affair or Ira is a nickname. At this point, Andrew's intuition kicks in. It is both, he realizes. Intuition, as the brilliant minds of history elucidated, does not flourish in a vacuum. It works best when worked hard. He does not have time to work hard. He will need time off from school to figure this out, especially with Tia watching over him like a mother hen. In fact, he will have to make it appear he is going to school when he is not.

'Hello, Bernice, it's Andrew Purser, Dr. Benson's patient.' On the phone, Bernice does not sound like Beatrice in the slightest. 'I was hoping to speak with Dr. Benson.'

Bernice gives him the usual about Benson being busy. She can leave the psychiatrist a message.

'I understand Dr. Benson is busy, of course, and we will see each other next week at our scheduled appointment. It may be in my best interest, though, to at least speak with her, even over the phone, before that. I will leave a message.'

Bernice would cut him off if he were someone else, or if he were rambling, but he can hear the solidity of each word as it leaves his mouth, followed by another.

'Go ahead, Andrew.'

'Please tell Ben – Dr. Benson – I am not sure with my med changes and sleep disruptions that I can make it to my classes this week. Feeling … off. Anyway, I don't want to skip school, but I feel kind of like school is adding to the stress … you know?' He does not want to ask outright for a note, which is what he needs. Bernice says she will pass on the message.

If Andrew does not get a note, well, so be it. It is not like he has never skipped school in his life. He should be at school right now, he realizes. It being a Thursday, Tia will be out until later, doing evening massages for pennies. Indentured slavery in Canada in the twenty-first century. *Disgusting.* And Tia participates with barely a sigh.

Focus!

On the closet's top shelf, under a half-dozen sweaters Tia rarely gets to wear in a city that never properly experiences winter, Andrew finds Tia's stash of keepsakes. It is in a plastic file folder, bright blue. Tia keeps it covered, does not intend for him to know it is there, but is not working particularly hard at hiding it. She does not believe he will look through it. And, until this moment, he has not. Right now, he must. He pulls out the folder and places it on the bed. Something twinges inside him. Maybe where his kidney lives, or his liver. Guilt. He is happy to know it is there, that he has not lost touch with that part of his body. Regardless of the necessity of his action, he loves Tia and this will hurt her. If she finds out. Which she need not. The guilt releases like a drop of water falling out of sight.

Black elastic bands wrap around each corner of the folder. He releases one and then the other. He does not trust himself to put things back in their right order, so he pulls out all of the contents at once. Paper scraps scatter like leaves onto the bedspread, the floor.

'Bugger!'

She will not notice. No one would notice, not even him. He places the pile on the bed, holding it tight until he believes it safe on the firm bedspread. Then he bends and gathers the fallen scraps. Receipts. *Why do people keep this shit?* People. Tia. *At least it is not boxes of it,* he tells himself. Gentle.

He starts at the beginning of the pile, one by one, each piece turned face down and placed to the left. A birthday card from her mother. A birthday card from him, last year. The same feeling in his midsection hits him again, is joined by warmth in his heart. He does love her. And she him. At least, she did. *Distraction,* all of this. He turns a third card

over and does not look inside. He can tell it is old, possibly from a childhood birthday. Then a letter. A piece of foolscap folded into eighths.

Dearest Tia,
I have gone on a treasure hunt. I will find you. Have a good day at
school.
Love, Pacifique
p.s. You are a light, the sun.

He stumbles and falls against the closet door. It jangles in the tracks
on the floor and comes loose. The door shudders with its new freedom,
echoing through the apartment like an alarm. *Shit!* wails inside his skull,
terror keeping his mouth closed.

Don't get caught, you stupid feck. Not now, with everything falling
into place.

He will not be discovered. It is all he needs to know. He gasps two
breaths. The air could be poison for all it fills him. Adrenaline shoots
through his major organs, leaving his hands buzzing and clumsy as he
attempts to put the items back in the folder. Everything he needs he
has found.

Just a moment, sir, we know nothing. This is evidence, certainly, but
without further analysis, it means nothing.

She got a bloody letter, from her bloody lover, right after you saw the
cunt shopping!

Mind your tongue! I will solve nothing if you continue to jump to
conclusions.

Andrew returns the folder to its hiding place, scrutinizes the sweaters
for more milliseconds than he feels he has, surveys the room. He hip-
checks the closet door into its tracks. A place for everything and everything in its place. Save for his desk. That is a disaster. Organized chaos.
A place to think. A place she will expect to find him when she comes
home. No, no, not if she comes home early, which she might.

Time. Time. Something about *time.*

Conjecture.

But why?

He cannot think here. He slips into runners and then, stroke of sanity, realizes he is supposed to be at school, which means, most of the time, wearing steel-toed boots in case of fieldwork. Pulls them on, clomps down the stairs, laces dangling, the letter's closing branded into his memory. *Love, Pacifique.*

Outside, he follows the shade. In the dark spaces under trees, his thoughts flow more easily, and the pavement does not send as much heat into his feet. No date. Not that a love letter needs a date. A thrown-together one would likely be without a date. Who is to say when the letter was sent? He assumes the letter came recently. Letters passing between ex-lovers' hands like money for drugs. The letter did not appear recent, though. In the same way Andrew knew it was a letter before opening it, he knows it is old. It has the wear of age that paper gets from simply existing in the outside world, not plastic-wrapped, not protected behind glass. The letter is not from last week, or this month. It has a history. Which is why it is in that folder. Memorabilia. Remember this. It is important.

Remember Pacifique.

He finds himself in a crosswalk, unprotected from the sun. He stops.

I think you've been taken for a spin, mate.

Tia told him she did not believe in Pacifique. She lied. Held a torch for a woman they both said was as real as the unicorn on Scotland's coat of arms. It was not pining, he realizes, the blare of a car horn as far away from him as he feels from his partner, his girlfriend. It was waiting.

Your wait is over, Tia. Your Pacifique has come back.

Chapter 28

Ira uses two recorders: video from a tripod-mounted digital camera on his desk and audio from a palm-sized machine on the small coffee table between them.

'Are you ready?'

Whatever *ready* means. 'Sure,' Tia says with a shrug.

He presses Record on both machines. 'Oh!' Ira removes his watch and places it beside the audio recorder. 'Ten minutes.'

Tia shrugs again. Her anxiety ebbs, then dissipates. 'Yup.'

'We will start now. Get comfortable in your chair, Tia. Find a position you can maintain for ten minutes with ease.'

She tucks her feet beneath her and adjusts the pillow at her back.

'I'm going to lead you through a simple meditation to relax you. Then I'll take you into trance.'

Tia remembers the meditation from years-ago sessions with Ira and from relaxation class at the hospital last year: close your eyes and imagine yourself in your favourite place. In hospital, she would take herself to a reading nook in a sunlit kitchen, and today she goes there again. It's not a place she knows; her family never had a sunlit kitchen with a reading nook. One that looked out onto green rolling fields, a lake or large pond in the distance ...

Ira holds out the box of tissues. She takes one to wipe the mess on her face, her hands, legs. The arm of the chair shines, too. She grabs another tissue and takes care of that.

'What the fuck? Why am I crying?' She searches for a clock. There isn't one, so she grabs Ira's watch: 11:16.

'It might be because of a woman named Pacifique?'

Tia stares into Ira's face, searching for deviousness, a hint he's been sent here. Maybe her mother staged an intervention. She stares and sees that it's just Ira, the same man who was here when she walked into the office, the same man she saw last week. The man she knew as a child.

Tia drops her feet to the floor, collapses over her legs, and retches. Ira moves a small garbage can from behind his chair and shoots it under Tia's head. Nothing comes but more tears. And a keening Tia hasn't heard herself make since nights alone in the hospital, heart breaking over the woman who left without saying goodbye.

The dry heaves slow. Tia gingerly sits back and places a protective hand over her belly, which feels empty even though nothing came up. Her body feels like it's made of light bulb filaments. She expects at any moment to rise to the ceiling and dissolve like fog. She raises a shoulder in an attempt at nonchalance and wipes one side of her face with her palm.

'Can I see?' she asks.

Ira stands, rolls his chair around the table, and sits down next to Tia. He turns the camera 180 degrees. He glances at Tia, and she nods, focused on the little screen now pointed her way. Ira presses Play.

※

Tia is alone at the beach. It's some time past noon, not yet five. Overcast, a low horizon. The ocean choppy, more pewter than blue. Tia has smelled autumn in the air a couple of times over recent weeks, and today it's clear the summer is ending. Bad news is always easier to deal with in the fall, in the winter, isn't it? Cold weather like an anesthetic. Or is it that bad news comes more often in the fall and winter and thus is expected? She's not even sure if this is bad news. It's confusing. Confounding. A mystery she has no hope of solving. Worse than what she used to think was the biggest mystery of all.

Ira wouldn't give her the tapes. He said he would make copies. He said he would do it right away.

The sand, unheated for as long as the sun has been hiding, is too cold, so Tia stands. Stares at the Pacific and pieces together what she saw. What she saw herself do. Heard herself say.

It started with Ira asking her where she was, as he had at their first appointment. She told him she was sitting in a sunlit kitchen nook. Then her expression on the video changed.

'Where are you going?' Tia said. Her eyes squeezed tight and she leaned forward. 'Don't do this again.' It was so clear she was talking to someone.

The tears came in seconds, and Tia's brows knitted like they do when she is confused or concentrating deeply. Pacifique. *I was speaking with Pacifique.* The spaces between her ribs tighten at the thought.

For a tiny moment after she and Ira watched the exchange on the camera screen, the world opened ahead of her, clear. As she thinks on it now at the beach, the questions land one on top of the other more quickly than she can answer them. The memory of what she watched and heard fades. What was it that she said? 'My promise ... '

'What promise?' Tia asked Ira after, as if he would know.

In the video, she had asked again, louder: 'Where are you going?' And then something like, 'That doesn't make sense. You can't go!' She and Pacifique had never had a conversation like that. She and Pacifique never fought. They hadn't had time. Or so she had thought.

Awake, she asked Ira, 'When was this? Where did you put me?'

'I don't know, Tia. It doesn't work that way. I don't pick. You pick.'

'I didn't pick that place. I don't know that place!' She was yelling.

'It's pretty clear you've gone to a place of high conflict. Your subconscious took you there. I just opened the door.'

'Why were we – ?'

Panic rose like fresh dough in her chest, blocking the airway. She tried to speak. She couldn't. Through the clanging anxiety, she heard another part of her brain saying, in rational, condescending tones, *Ira cannot help you.* A cord pulled taut and the pressure in her chest squeezed her heart so hard she coughed, desperate against the pain.

'Look at me, Tia.' Ira pointed at his eyes. 'Look at me. I'm right here. You're safe.'

She was, of course. Anxiety the least productive of all emotions. Meaningless, melodramatic, and tiresome.

'The only way to find out where you went in hypnosis today is to go back.'

'I can't do that again.'

A hand in her stomach curled into a fist. *If you don't go back*, a voice said behind her ear, *you won't see her again.*

'This is going to get harder before it gets easier, Tia.' His tone no longer held the softness of the avuncular sympathy he'd been cultivating for most of the session.

Tia squinted. 'Do you think I shouldn't?'

'Hypnotherapy is not for everyone.'

'You said it was!' Could no one be reliable?

Ira looked away. If he had been wearing glasses, he would have taken them off and cleaned them with the corner of his shirt. He studied the blunt-tipped fingers in his lap for a moment, then looked out the window.

'Hypnotherapy is not for everyone,' he repeated. He spoke to the window, to the harbour. 'You might go somewhere you don't want to go.'

Tia sneered despite herself. Ira's warmth and light had disappeared. He was reminding her very much of her hospital shrink.

'You said it yourself, Tia: the brain is a powerful machine of cognition and forgetting,' he went on. 'Sometimes we forget because remembering is so much worse. Hypnotherapy can take us places we were never meant to go.' Ira cleared his throat. His focus flickered off Tia's face to her left ear, the wall behind her. He dropped his eyes again.

'Ignorance is bliss?' Tia blurted, then cringed.

Ira looked up. A hint of ease had returned to his face. 'Do you know the whole quote?'

Tia shook her head.

'"Where ignorance is bliss, 'tis folly to be wise." Everyone always just says the first bit.' He laughed then, or what could have been called laughter if it had come from a man who didn't look on the verge of crying.

'Is that true?'

'So I've been told,' he said.

Tia left without making an appointment; instead, she had Ira's guarantee he would get her the tapes. Now she wanders on the beach, runners half-full of sand, sea silent. She has been on this stretch of beach before, the night of the bonfire, when Pacifique disappeared and the man in the Cowichan sweater startled her. Tia had been close to angry then, angry about Pacifique's penchant for vanishing.

Tia remembers now what Pacifique had said once they got home that night: 'Promise me you will remember ... '

In the video, Tia asked, 'My promise?' The promise she forgot. She had promised she would remember. She had broken her promise.

Tia whispers to the surf, 'I never forgot you, Pacifique. I swear.' And then: 'Pacifique!'

The grey swallows her shout with a gulp.

'Pacifique!' she tries again, louder.

She needs a canyon, wishes for Echo to return her words – any response, however fake, better than this silence. Tia straightens, stacks vertebra on top of vertebra, contracts her abdominals, and slowly exhales. Empties all air. Diaphragm engaged, she fills her lungs, her stomach, every space with oxygen, carbon dioxide, nitrogen, water, until her ribs and the intercostal muscles protest. When the air comes out, there's no name attached to the scream, just a wordless cry, closer to a roar than a shout, the edges guttural. The yell disappears into the sky and Tia slumps, spine curved into a C, silent.

Chapter 29

Tia's Converse sneaker – size nine, so big for a woman, he's often thought – floats into his peripheral vision a moment before his shoulder connects with hers. They have run into each other on the sidewalk outside their apartment building.

'Sor–'

He cuts off the apology and checks his own feet. Boots. He does not know exactly what time it is but he thinks he is safe. The sun slants on that nearly fall angle that befits five o'clock. Some days he is home by four, sometimes six. He is fine. Fine. Everything is fine.

'I have something to tell you,' Tia says.

He should not have looked through her things. He should have trusted that she would tell him in her own time. The dark circles under Tia's eyes have deepened. She always looks underslept. Today she looks like she does not know what the word *sleep* means.

Not you, too, Tia.

Chin up, mate. You'll get tail on the inside if you're locked up at the same time again.

Pervert.

He nods. Do not give anything away.

'I am seeing someone,' she says.

Yes. You are. *I will fight for you.* This, new. And right. What kind of man lets his girlfriend waltz off with some bimbo lesbo with a nice ass?

Tia shakes her head, grabs both nostrils between thumb and forefinger, shakes the button nose one, two, three times. Releases her hand, uses it to wipe her upper lip. It is an unsavoury habit, one she is doing more often. Sniffs. She has done a lot of crying today. The whites of her eyes are pink. 'For the dreams.'

'The dreams?'

She does the awful nose thing again. 'The terrors. The bad dreams. The thing that woke us.'

Dreams. Not the right word for that bit of nonsense. He has never been one for nightmares. Sleeping ones, anyway. He sees enough horror while awake, thank you very much.

'Ira,' he says.

Bugger!

Keep your bloody trap shut.

'Yes!' She raises her chin a notch, and the dark circles lighten, catching the sun. 'You remember.'

In that moment, he does. She mentioned him shortly after she was discharged, something about wanting his help while she was hospitalized. She did not mention him again. 'Ira' familiar after all.

'He still works, doing the sleep stuff. So I saw him. Twice now. I'm sorry. It was the phone call that morning. I lied. I'm really sorry.'

She is telling the truth now. But what about – 'Pacifique?'

Fucking Christ, are you mental?

Her head moves back. *Ah.* She closes her mouth.

'Sorry.' He tries again. 'I mean, did you talk about Pacifique? Too. As well.'

'Why would we do that?'

He got away with a lot of lying to his mother by playing defence. A dead giveaway. 'I thought she was also in the dreams.'

'No. Never. They're terrors, Andrew.'

He waits for her to grab her nose again. She does not. A gust off the ocean carries down their street and snakes through his jacket.

'Pacifique was good,' she says.

The lie lives here somewhere. The meat of it.

'She was always a good thing,' Tia says. 'Totally unrelated.'

They did talk about Pacifique. So she is not telling him, big deal. She has not delivered herself of her delusion. *Call the papers!* Hell, he saw Beatrice the other day. Tia came clean on one thing, holds the rest to her chest. Fair enough. The guilt has subsided. It is sweet of Tia to come clean about the Ira fellow. It would be sweeter if she cut the bullshit entirely.

'Well,' he says, 'I am freezing. Shall we?'

'You're not mad.'

'No,' he says. He opens the gate for her, closes it behind them.

Tia veers left. 'Do you think I should do something about these? It's cold. Is it too cold?' She speaks to the plants bordering the picket fence, its paint peeling.

I will take care of that next summer.

Good plan, mate, but you know it's highly unlikely you'll be around to do anything of the sort.

Fuck you. We will sort it out.

Good luck.

'I have no idea.'

Tia's head snaps left. 'You are mad.'

'No, I'm really not. Sorry. I just … I do not know a thing about gardening. Ask Shirley.'

Tia sighs. More things that will never happen.

✳

The next fourteen hours pass with difficulty. Questions about his appointment with Benson. Answers provided in a tone he has never used with Tia. Shirk the bristling that builds when she asks about meds. No, no new meds. Just different dosages. Yes, he filled the prescription. That should go without saying, so why does she ask? Trust gone, like everything else. *You lie, I lie. Seems fair.* Tia retires to bed early, says the psychologist tired her out – 'I bet he did,' Andrew says, and Tia shoots him a look dripping with disdain. Love replaced. It happens that quickly, does it? *Snarl at me all you want, Tia, I will take it. You will not be snarling when*

I confront you with all I know.

Andrew sits at his computer. Fights the urge to do some research. Can Pacifique be found online? Unlikely. There are those who have escaped the clutches of Google. She would be one of them. Plus, he must mind his surroundings. He forces himself into a game and the hours drift by. No dead-weight antipsychotics on board to lull him into complacency. His brain illuminated. The source of light itself. The path ahead clear, shiny.

✳

'I have an exam today and I haven't studied, so I'm off.'

Tia stands next to the bed, wearing a rain jacket. He does not remember going to sleep.

'You should get up,' she says. 'You'll be late for school.'

He grunts his assent. She does not move. A thousand forgotten dreams swirl in his brain. 'I'm up, I'm up,' he says through the gravel in his throat.

Tia hesitates, then bends down. The peck on his cheek as cold as if it were coming from a stranger. He engages the muscles in his face that create a smile. All the world a stage. Tia exits.

He does not rush. The calm he could not find last night comes to him this morning. Why rush? The time is right. He must simply tread the road laid out for him and he will find the answers he seeks. He pushes for a moment. Comes upon ... nothing. A haze. Something like the fog that buries their neighbourhood some mornings. No matter. He is not meant to know, not yet. He showers, taking special care with everything that smells. Shaves with a new razor. He dresses for school: boxer briefs, jeans, soft cotton undershirt, plaid button-up. Everything fresh, clean from the closet, shirts coming unfolded with hospital-corner creases at the appropriate places. He flosses his teeth mindfully. Brushes in the same way. No manic gum-slicing today. Decides he cannot risk taking care of the blackheads for fear of leaving the house with a drunkard-red nose. His hair, longer than it has been in a while, behaves under his hands. It looks not bad. Finally, he addresses his face as a whole. He does not look like a man gone mad. He could be handsome. He does not really know. Tia thinks so – thought so. Has said terribly untrue things to him, usually post-orgasm.

'You are the only man who has ever understood me,' she would say before falling asleep. 'Don't you know how beautiful you are?'

He is not the first and he will not be the last man to fall under the wiles of a woman. How to maintain control when the delivery is so ... honest? *I love you* three words he never wants to hear again.

When he checks the clock, his class has already been in session for a half-hour. Tia has been gone two hours. He knew about the exam, that is truth. She is likely sitting for the written portion now. In an hour, they will have a short break. Then she will do the practical part. She may not ace it like she usually does, having not studied, but she will do well. By Christmas, she will be a registered massage therapist. Good for her. He already ordered her graduation present – a gorgeous early-edition copy of *Gray's Anatomy* that someone was selling for a reasonable price on eBay. Stupid: both the seller who parted with this piece of history for a fraction of its value and he who thought the gift's recipient had gotten over her ex.

The folder has not been moved. He was certain Tia would have gone in there at some point since he mentioned seeing Pacifique at the grocery store. Or since seeing that Ira character. Perhaps she has memorized her memorabilia and needs no refresher. How many times did she finger these pieces of paper while he sat in the next room gaming, while he worked his ass off as an electrician's apprentice, a trade that would one day make them a lot of money? Massage therapy a perfectly fine occupation, as long as you could do it. So much touching of people, all day, serving, serving, serving the needs of others. Tia is too empathetic for the job. She will burn out in two years. Less.

Somebody woke up on the wrong side of the bed today.

Shut up.

He ignores the letter. He knows the letter. The cards are in the same order. The bulk of the folder contains papers, also loose-leaf, not folded. Sheets joined with a large white paperclip. He separates the sheaf from its neighbours, laying the loose sheets behind it to the left, cards and other junk in front of it to the right.

Pacifique
I met Pacifique on a Tuesday in February. It had snowed, heavy, wet, freezing snow and the transformer down the street blew. I took to the streets. Later I understood it was to find her, to be found by her. I remember the snow soaked my Chucks and I thanked my wool socks. I didn't turn around. Everything felt right. Even then, before we met.

I fell at Bastion Square and there she was. She wore these white gloves with mother-of-pearl buttons. Her hair shone. She had purple eyes. Violet. Amethyst. I'm still not sure how to describe the colour. Wide-set, oval-shaped. She had orange freckles across her nose and high cheekbones. She was the most beautiful person I had ever seen. And me on my ass. She made like she knew me, had her hand on my back right away. I suppose it was flirting. I didn't mind. I liked it. As soon as I felt her hand on my lower back, I wanted more. I wanted her hands everywhere. I had never felt this way about anyone.

Andrew puts down the pages.
It's like reading her bloody diary.
Curiosity comes in two sizes, one much heavier to bear. Can he carry the shame, the heartache, that will come with knowing every last detail?
More importantly, a smarter part of him cuts in, *does it suit your purposes?*
No. It does not.
He loosens his grip.
Skip the naughty bits, sure, but everything else you're lookin' for's right there. Clues.

Tia blabbed on and on about Pacifique for most of their early acquaintance, but hell if he can remember any details.

Read it.

No time.

You got time. You got all day.

I must assume I have very little time. I must work as efficiently as possible.

Pussy.

'Grah!' Andrew drops the papers on the bed and grabs his head with both hands. 'Leave me the fuck alone, will you? I don't have time for this shit.'

Sorry, mate.

Andrew exhales. Inhales. Releases his head.

Focus, says another whisper.

Thank you.

Yes. Focus. Clues. It *is* all here. He notes which of the discarded scraps came before and which came after the writing, and returns them to their rightful spots in the blue folder. He puts the file where it belongs, arranges the sweaters, yes, all is well, nothing out of place. Except for what lies on the bed, waiting. An absence that will go unnoticed. For now. He slides the mirrored door, hiding his handiwork, revealing his side of the closet. He removes his top as carefully as he put it on and returns it as carefully as he pulled it out. Plaid shirt on a hanger with the others, arranged by colour, then type. The closet so well laid out that anyone in the system would be proud. *Yes, sir, I keep my locker clean.* His own mother's closet a departure from what else he has seen in girls' closets: tidy, arranged, like his, in order, albeit an order he does not comprehend. Tia's side a mess of … woman. A mishmash of colour, items, stuff on the floor, and clothes he has never seen her wear, things she could not possibly fit into. A few months ago, he asked what the billowing thing was stuffed into the far corner, its hem collecting dust bunnies like a child in a pet store.

'My grad dress,' she said.

'Grad? Grade 12?'

'Yes.'

'That was a long time ago.'

'It's a beautiful dress. I'll wear it again sometime.'

'The next time you graduate from high school.'

Her look enough to darken the whole room. 'I'll repurpose it. Tear it up, make it into something new. My aunt spent hours on that dress. Should I throw it away?'

Tia did not take his bullshit. Or anyone else's, which is why she got into hospital in the first place. She learned her place, not the lesson. At first, he liked having someone who could sometimes meet him on his level. Almost smart enough. He did not want a woman who was smart enough. Had to keep on top, always. He had learned that, at boarding school. Boarding school, military school. He so rarely called it military school but that is what it was. Discipline. Control. Power.

'How would you repurpose it? You do not sew.'

'You're exasperating,' she said, and left the room.

That bloody dress is still there. She paid half the rent, what could he say? She was probably holding on to the dress to wear with Pacifique. The thing would look ridiculous. It would look terrible on Tia now, although he had seen pictures of her at seventeen, when she was smaller, younger. With a young man who looked as geeky as Andrew had at the same age. The photo gave him comfort. Tia looked sweet, all belled up for the ball. Now it left him irritated. Why would she date a man who could not even wear a suit with dignity? Why would she not grow up and give the dress to someone who would actually wear it? Or at least store it somewhere other than in his closet.

Time's a wastin', mate.

Shit.

He removes his undershirt, folds it in six, returns it to the top of the pile on the shelf. Hangs his jeans on a hanger, throws the boxers into the laundry hamper. Shuffles the pile so they fall underneath older clothes, in case Tia remembers what was on top this morning.

Paranoid.

Never be too careful.

He dresses again, this time in pyjamas. Double-checks the door is locked. Then takes his boots and drops them from knee height. Heads for bed.

Chapter 30

She pockets her phone and puts the key in the lock. Ira called. She will grab the Pacifique story and go straight to his office. The door hits something. Tia pushes and trips over a workboot in the foyer.

'Andrew?' she calls. Nothing.

The thing she hit is the second boot. Andrew's sneakers are on the shoe rack. She grabs the boots, puts them in their place. His desk is empty. The apartment feels empty.

'Andrew?' she says again, louder.

She struggles with her high-tops. The second foot releases with a *schlupp* and the sock stays behind. It is a rubber-boot day, but she doesn't have rubber boots. Her bare foot is pruned and pink. She steps off the doormat onto the hardwood, drops her bag. The thump reverberates through the floor. She waits and listens to a silence that is too full, too quiet. Andrew is here. She enters the bedroom and finds him in bed, sleeping. *Shit*. If she can sneak past him, she can get the pages without waking him. The closet is open on his side. She takes another look at the man in their bed: he is more prone-with-eyes-shut than sleeping.

'Andrew,' she says, and lays three fingers on his arm.

'Mmm,' he says. Not asleep.

'Honey, it's after noon. Have you been sleeping this whole time?'

'Hmmm?'

She swallows the sigh. 'I said, it's after noon.'

He rolls over with a slowness verging on vaudevillian. Flutters his eyelids. Looks beyond her and then at her, his gaze clear like the harbour on a windless, winter day. Impassive.

'Is it? Sleeping. Yes, I've been sleeping.'

He rubs away imaginary sleep, scratches his scalp. His thinking tic, used on purpose.

Tia fights against the anger that roils in her stomach. 'You missed school.'

'I know. I got up to go, left, but I could barely stand. These new meds are kicking my ass. So I called in sick.'

'Did you talk to Benson?'

His composure falters. 'Yeah. Well, no. I left a message.'

'Andrew.'

'It's fine, Tia, don't worry about it.'

'Whatever.'

He doesn't get up. Stays lying there, covers pulled to his armpits, one hand shoved under the pillow. 'What are you doing home?'

'The exam went fine, thanks for asking.'

'So you get the afternoon off?'

'No. I'm just home quick. We have a thing this afternoon. I wanted to drop off my books.'

'I am happy to hear about the exam. When will you find out your grade?'

These past weeks have been one first after another.

'Next week.' Let's see what happens when she says, 'I don't need to go to school. Let's get you up and doing something. If you sleep all day, you won't sleep tonight. You need to power through the drugs.'

'No, no, go to school.'

Too quick.

'I'll get up.'

'That's what you said this morning.'

'No offence, Tia, but your experience of antipsychotics is limited. You know I take four times the amount you ever did. And this new one, it's a doozy.'

'You said there wasn't a new one.'

'I mean the newest one. Remember? Last time I changed meds. This time Benson's changed the dose. It's like I'm starting all over again.'

He's sure, crafted. Whatever he's on – new drug, new dosage, she's not sure what to believe – it's not slowing him down.

'I'm gonna be straight with you,' she says. 'I don't think you're going to school today. And that's fine. You called, you talked to Benson. Clearly you don't want me here, so I'll go.' She turns.

'Tia!'

She pauses.

'Tia,' he says.

'I'm not mad,' she says to the doorway.

She knows what she must say. *Don't be a coward*. She turns. He leans on one elbow. His brow furrows.

'You see it, don't you?' she asks. 'How it's falling apart?'

His eyes sparkle. He nods.

'So I won't fight with you,' says Tia.

'You are giving up.'

'That's not what I said.'

'That's what it sounds like.'

'I said I won't fight with you.'

'We are not fighting,' he says. 'We are discussing.'

Stifle the yell that struggles to escape. If she opens her mouth, it will come out. Say nothing.

'Please come back,' he says.

'I have to go.'

'Please come back.'

'What are you talking about?'

'Don't leave me.'

'Andrew … '

'Not yet. We will talk and we will figure this out.'

'I'm tired, Andrew.'

'I know. Me too. But please promise you will come back and we will talk.'

'Of course I'll come back. I'll be here after school. Is that what you mean? I'm not, like, moving out or something.'

The words float into the universe. Moving out. Leaving. It is a blunt spoon looking for purchase on the back of her heart. Digging.

'Yes. Tonight. Come back.'

'Of course. Now I really have to go. The thing. At the school.'

'Yes. Absolutely,' he says.

He knows she has no intention of going to school, but he does not appear to mind. What treachery is this? *Off his meds.* Just plain off. No refills, no new prescription, no call to Benson. *For how long? Why am I only seeing it now?*

'I have to go. Do you want a kiss?' Not what she expected she would say.

He considers this. 'Yes,' he says, and his brows unlock. His ears shift back.

She remembers that look, feels it reflected on her face. One foot in front of the other, chilled from damp and stasis. She takes his face in her hand and he flinches. His face the sun, her fingers ice. Lips brush his smooth upper lip – he shaved today – and she closes her eyes. *Upstairs, downstairs* she remembers an older girl in high school calling it, the way the four lips stack one on top of the other. He tastes like Andrew, and something else. Something musky and moist like a river after the spring melt. The fuzziness of his ever-present dry mouth replaced with saliva she forgot he had.

'You're beautiful,' she says.

He shrinks. Wipes his chin with the nearest corner of sheet and plasters on a plastic smile. 'See ya.'

On the way out, she grabs a couple of mismatched socks sticking out of her dresser's overstuffed top drawer. Tries to rub blood into her numb feet with the new socks, gives up. Shoves the dry feet into wet shoes. Hefts her bag, remembers the books, pulls them out. Does she have everything? No. That's fine, she'll see Ira without the story. Her memory will have to serve.

✳

A disc sits on Ira's desk. She reaches for it, pauses. Ira nods.

'Video file and audio file both on there. Yours to keep. Do with as you will.'

'Thank you.' Tia takes a straight-backed wooden seat opposite Ira. No cozy armchair today, apparently.

'I'm sorry if I worried you with my phone call today. Something has come up.'

'Are you okay?' Cancer. He has cancer. Or, no. 'Am I being fired?'

'You were always so astute, Tia. That hasn't changed.'

'You want to stop seeing me? Already?'

'Let me tell you why. I hope you will understand once I explain. Why it's best. I meant to hit the punchline last but I should have been prepared.' A wry smile flashes across his face. 'It's a long story.'

'I have time.' *All the time in the world, Ira, remember?*

'Thank you.'

Ira takes a deep breath. Cups a hand around his recreated jaw, massages the stubble on his chin. Andrew shaved this morning, he did not.

'Something twigged for me during our last appointment. I went to my archives and found your file. Found something ... interesting. Don't you hate that word?'

Tia stares.

'Sorry. I'll back up. When your parents first brought you to me – your mother, in truth, but when we would have our meetings together, it would often be both your parents who came – '

'My parents ... '

'I often met with the parents of my patients, if the parents were in the picture.'

Of course, she remembers that.

'Your mother was especially concerned about your mental health.'

Huh.

'Although that wasn't a term we used then. Your mother likely would have been hurt to hear me suggest you had "mental" problems.' Ira's square fingers create air quotes.

Why don't they have you in the loony bin, Ira?

'In my view, however, it was a question of mental health. Something was awry with your brain, and it was affecting your daily life. Your mother brought you in with two chief concerns: your night terrors and your imaginary friend.'

'My imaginary friend?'

'You don't remember.'

'No. I mean, I guess I had, like, dolls and bears and toys that I talked to.'

'There was a full-blown imaginary friend in your life. A child, a human, if you will. Most children talk to their toys, and their toys talk back. That's pretty standard. A lot of children have imaginary friends. You were not special in that regard either.'

'Oh.'

Ira laughs. 'Sorry to burst the special bubble.'

'It's a drag being special.'

'Your mother thought so, too. She thought your terrors and your imaginary friend needed to ... go.'

'And you agreed?'

Ira stops, mouth half-open.

'Sorry.'

'No problem. Like I said, a bit of a long story.'

'Right.' Tia's sit bones dig into the wooden chair. 'Is part of the long story sitting in these chairs?'

'Ah. No, sorry. We can sit wherever you like. The desk is not required for this story.'

'It's nice over there,' says Tia, and nods at the armchair under the window.

Ira stands, spins his chair, pushes it from behind the desk. Tia rises from the hard chair, her coccyx breathing thanks, and drops into the squishy armchair. Much better.

'Give me my popcorn, Mr. DeMille,' Tia says. 'I'm ready for my long story.'

Ira smiles, mouth closed, lines on either side of his face cracking and breaking into sixty years of smiling. 'Thanks for coming in today, Tia, really. You are a light.'

You are a light, the sun. Tears sting, and Tia blinks several times fast.

'Good?'

She nods.

'Where was I?'

'Night terrors and imaginary friend equal crazy.'

He gives her a look.

'I can use that word. I'm certifiable.'

'You're not certifiable. What good does it do to think of yourself that way?'

'I was. I was crazy.' *I was in love with an imaginary woman.*

Ira places a hand on his hip. 'So they say.'

'So they say. They never really understood.'

'There are some amazing people working over there' – Ira bobs his head west – 'but psychiatry has only one set of answers.'

That's a nice way of putting it. 'Tell me your story. I'll tell you about the hospital another time. Over coffee!'

Ira doesn't share her light tone. 'The story. Yes.'

'Night terrors plus – '

'Mental health. When I took you through hypnosis, you mentioned Pacifique. And that's what twigged. I know Pacifique.'

What?

'I know of her, I should say. Knew of her. Her name was in your file. She was your imaginary friend, when you were little, when you were first here.'

'No. No, what? Look, I don't remember an imaginary friend.'

'I'll explain.'

'I remember Pacifique. I just met her. In February of last year, for the first time. Or, well, met, fantasized, I don't know. The psychosis. That was Pacifique.'

'Pacifique is not a common name. I've never heard anyone but you mention a Pacifique.'

'Yeah, I know it's a weird name. She's the only Pacifique I know, too. Ira, tell me the story because I'm really fucking confused.'

'And angry,' he says, voice soft.

God, why does he do this? She starts to cry.

'I'll tell the rest of the story right now, all of it. If it gets too much, tell me to stop. You can cry, you can shout at me, whatever you need to do. Does that sound okay?'

No. None of this sounds okay. She nods.

Ira takes a deep breath, a diver going under. 'Your mother and I agreed the terrors and the imaginary friend should be addressed. We disagreed on an important point: your mother thought the two were related. I thought they were separate. Turns out your mother was right and I was wrong. At first, we focused on the night terrors. T. Rex, that kind of thing. I didn't worry too much about your imaginary friend because I figured she'd go away on her own, you'd grow out of her. The night terrors, being so, well, terrible, were my first priority. But your imaginary friend took a greater hold of you. Pacifique was around all the time.'

Tia flinches.

'I'd hear from your mother that you'd missed school because you were off with her. That you'd come home late, talking of adventures. One night she got a call from another mother frantic because you'd wandered off from a birthday party. "Pacifique came to get me," you told your mother. She spanked you. She was furious.'

Tia remembers an often-furious mother. Working more than full-time, thrown into motherhood by accident. As accidental as using the rhythm method for birth control can be, Tia said to her at fifteen. The slap Tia expected when she saw the flare of anger in her mother's face didn't come, the anger glazed over with a sadness that kicked a piece from Tia's teenage heart.

'She said more of my focus in our sessions needed to be on this Pacifique girl, that you were being bullied at school, that kids had started saying things.'

Shilo, whose mother had told her Tia was seeing Ira. Tia says, 'You're crazy.'

'Yes, they said that. You got fewer invitations to birthday parties, fewer kids dropped by. The thing was, you weren't bothered by any of it. You and Pacifique had such a great time together. It's all in my notes, these epic tales. I wrote them down, for the record, but most I discounted as fantasy. When you said you went swimming in the ocean, for example, in the winter, I didn't believe you. In the meeting with your parents, however, your mother told me you'd come home with wet hair, "verging on hypothermic."' Air quotes again. 'And I thought, shit, this is pretty serious. I got on board. I decided that you and Pacifique needed to integrate.

'Integration is a dated practice, but the idea is that we naturally have a lot of selves, and that to be complete, we integrate these selves into a fully functioning human. Healthy people are integrated. Nothing has to *happen*, it's just the way it is. If there's trouble, sometimes the selves come apart. When there's big trouble – like mental illness – for example, this coming-apart affects a person's ability to live the life they're supposed to. Be it the one they want, which is what my focus usually is, or the one society wants for them, which is where your mother comes in. And me. Your mother thought right away – and eventually I joined her in thinking – Pacifique needed to go. Inside. She was affecting your ability to live your life.

'It didn't take long. Only a few sessions, which surprised me, given how much trouble we'd had with your night terrors. Then your mother called me, after the session in which I asked you about Pacifique and you said, "Who?" It was phenomenal. Anyway, your mother. She called me in a state and she said, "Jo, Pacifique is gone, which is great, thank you." In this sort of *I'm saying thank you but I hate you* kind of tone.'

Tia laughs. She knows it.

'She said she spent the night in emergency with you because you had the worst terror she'd ever seen. She couldn't wake you. You were screaming and sweating, and she didn't know what to do, she had to call an ambulance. She fired me. She said, and I have this written down, it's a quote, "I don't know what you're doing over there with my little girl, but you won't be doing it anymore." She hung up. I didn't charge for your last session, but your mother, so organized, had paid already. I tried calling. It was no use. I had made a very big mistake. I knew then, for sure, that your imaginary friend and the terrors were related, and that I had done you a disservice by this so-called integration. I don't do integration therapy anymore. I think it's fundamentally flawed. I made a mistake, Tia, and I'm sorry. When Janey said you'd called, all of this came rushing back, but I had forgotten her name, your friend. Pacifique.'

Tia waits. Ira says no more. 'That's it? That's the story?'

'Yes.'

'So Pacifique was my imaginary friend and you did the integration therapy wrong and she came back?'

'No. I mean, sure, possibly. Who's to say? I'm no expert.'

'I thought you were.'

'Anybody who claims to be an expert in matters of the brain, the spirit, is lying. Or deluded. Or both.'

'The spirit?'

'Integration theory has brokenness at its core. It claims we are broken and we need to be fixed. To suggest a child who has an imaginary friend is broken is highly problematic. I have changed my perspective on the therapy since I used it. I didn't consider it as a "brokenness" theory back then. I do now. And you, Tia, are a prime case study. You are the first person to come back to me and tell me your imaginary friend returned to you. I watched her, Pacifique, all grown-up, with you.'

'You really think it's the same person – imaginary friend.'

'I do. Why are you resisting this? You expect to have two different imaginary friends with the same name?'

'I'm sure it happens.'

'Of course. I remember one kid who had three imaginary Freds: a little boy, a dragon, and a piece of toast. It became Toast Fred, Dragon Fred, Friend Fred. Friend Fred was a silly nickname, because the boy's r's hadn't come in yet, and I'd often have to clarify which Fred he meant. Anyway. Sorry.'

Tia laughs. 'See, I can have two Pacifiques.'

'I don't think you do. I think it's the same one.'

'So ... what's the new therapy? Instead of integration?'

'For you?'

'Well, yeah.'

'From me, none. I'm firing you, remember?' He says it with a sad smile, an apology.

'Oh, right. Okay, well, what the fuck do I do then?'

'Do you want to rid yourself of Pacifique?'

'Don't ask me that.'

'I just did.'

The tears come back. 'Please don't.'

'It's okay if you want to say yes.'

'I don't.' Two steps forward, four hundred and some back. 'I don't want to say yes.'

'What do you want to say?'

'No. I want to say no. I don't want to get rid of Pacifique.'

Ira's eyes sparkle.

'Oh my god!' she says. 'Why are you crying?' Tia sniffs hard, blinks, and wipes a hand across her face.

'My own fucked-up shit, Tia. I never could quite shake the feeling that I failed you, all those years ago. You've managed to forgive the mistakes I may have made. I appreciate that.'

'I don't know what you mean.'

'I know. You don't have to. I'm not crying from being upset. I'm happy. Quite happy, in fact.'

'And me? What do I do?'

Ira shakes his head. 'I don't have a single suggestion for you. I know that's a cop-out. But pretending I can actually help you would be much worse.'

'I can figure this out on my own.'

'Exactly.'

'Somehow.'

'Trust. It's in there. It's always been in there. You know yourself better than anyone.'

'I really don't.'

Ira doesn't respond.

'I'll go now,' she says. 'I've been here forever.'

Ira looks at his watch. 'It's been a very long time, and only twenty minutes. Thank you for coming in.'

Twenty minutes? Tia stands. Her legs unfold, every joint and muscle in place. 'So long?'

'Yes. So long.'

Ira walks her to the door. He palms the doorknob.

'Wait,' Tia says.

Ira drops his hand from the doorknob and opens his arms. The hug is warm and sad. It's the first time she has ever been this close to Ira, and it will be the last.

Chapter 31

When he and Tia moved in together, they talked other neighbourhoods – Fernwood, downtown, Oak Bay – but looked at only one place, the big-windowed, utilities-included, one-bedroom apartment they share in Fairfield. Can they get out of their lease? Can he manage the rent on his own? Certainly not. His disability cheque keeps him in video games. It will not keep him in house.

If Tia wants to leave, let her worry about the bloody lease.

I am not going to be a child about this. We are adults. It is a simple legal matter and we will sort it out. I am getting ahead of myself, anyway. We will discuss this misunderstanding and move forward, together.

There ain't no misunderstanding. That's the problem. It's all pretty darn clear from here.

From there? Where is there exactly?

Everywhere. I see it all. And you do, too. Don't pretend you don't.

Shh. Please. Calm in the face of a storm, that is the measure of a man.

Whatever you say.

Living in Fairfield, a small neighbourhood in a small city, means they reside mere blocks from Tia's former house, a diminutive bungalow near the end of south Quadra. Andrew finds himself here today. At the end of this block is Beacon Hill Park. The ocean. In another life, Tia lived here with two other young women.

Maybe that's when she got a taste of the poontang.

You are disgusting.

Just 'cause you don't like doing it. Bloody fun, diving into that pie. Tia always liked it. A lot. Bet she got loads of it before your lazy ass came plodding along.

Andrew digs his fingernails into his palm. The house lies in the shadow of an ugly several-storey apartment building. Tia told him in hospital about rushing out to find Pacifique one day, forgetting something, and leaving her bag on the boulevard. She was gone sixty seconds, less, and still the bag had disappeared. She got it back a few hours later at the police station.

'All they took was my cash, my granola bar, and my smokes. It was somebody hungry, someone living in the park.'

'Your smokes.'

'Yeah.'

'You smoked. Before the hospital.'

'I did.'

'That is a filthy habit.'

'Oh, really? You know, you're the first person I've ever heard say that.'

He has not thought of that moment in months, more. It was early in their acquaintance and the memory would have been lost to time if he had left it much longer. By that maple over there is likely where she dropped her bag, and the opportunist, on a bicycle most definitely, came up this driveway, snagged it, and disappeared like a ghost into the park. Half a minute. That is all he needed. What could Andrew find in that park? A hundred hungry men playing cards, betting with cigarettes stolen from thoughtless women.

You look like a stalker standing here. Go.

North. He tries to imagine the route Tia took to Bastion Square. No snow today. No night quiet. The breeze brisk, touched with notes of leaves going to rot. Under a frozen sky, Tia would have taken the prettiest route. No sun or traffic to contend with. He turns west at Humboldt and avoids looking at the looming nunnery that occupies most of the block. Cannot ignore the billow of white. A bride on the steps of the 140-year-old building, surrounded by a gaggle of girls in pink dresses. Short. The requisite fat one, squeezed in. The requisite tattooed one, complete with long black hair. He squints. No, she's white, and too tall, and, although the woman has gams good enough for the brow-raising hem, they are not the ones he saw at the grocery store. A man hefts a camera the size of a typewriter in his left hand, gestures with his right. Bends and fiddles with the bottom of the bridal gown. The groom and his men nowhere.

What a job.

At least he's got one.

He does not have an ingrate barrelling in on every private moment.

What've I got to be grateful for? It's been a mindfuck-a-minute these days and I don't like it.

You and me both.

The end of the block the beginning of downtown's condo mania. All directions equally ugly. Tia would have avoided Douglas. He veers right, huffs a bit on the slope, lefts at the corner, crosses Douglas. Government workers on coffee breaks, muffins, cigarettes, paper bags, murses, the same attempt-at-upscale dress pants, the same salmon-pink dress shirt. A couple of women wearing sneakers over nylons. A look that he and Tia agreed, many moons ago, should be outlawed. They giggled, grabbed each other, and, when safely out of earshot, laughed hard, collapsing over their knees. He scoots along Courtney, away from the memory, zig-zags a couple of times, and there it is. Bastion Square. Looking the same as it has since he can remember. She walked these cobblestones, unaware that her life would turn on its head. It started with a fall, ended with a fall. *Curious.* Propelled by intention, she slipped. And then Pacifique appeared, on these steps here. Andrew sits. On his right, on the other side of the next railing, sits a man wearing the shoes Tia likes, Converse, dark blue jeans rolled above his ankles, and an army jacket with a Misfits patch the size of a newspaper page on the back. Black plastic-rimmed glasses, a pageboy hat. Smoking.

'Excuse me,' says Andrew.

Shut it. What are you doing?

The man does not respond. Does not seem to have heard.

Leave him.

'Sir?' Louder. 'Excuse me, can I ask you a question?'

The man turns. Interrupted from whatever thoughts he brought with him to the square. Older than his outfit might suggest. At least forty. His face is expressionless.

'I wonder if you know of a nightclub that once operated in these parts. Called Nightclub.' Andrew gestures toward the blue bridge. 'At the end of the block.'

The man appraises him. 'Yeah,' he says. Still that blank face.

'Yeah? You sure?'

This gets a twitch from the stranger. 'Yeah. But years ago. Long time.'

'Where exactly?'

The man sighs, glances at the cigarette wasting away between his fingers. 'Just where you said. In the last building, the basement.' He turns away.

See. Worth bothering the nice punk man.

'Thank you,' says Andrew, and the man, staring straight ahead, gives the slightest of nods.

Andrew stumbles on the steps in his rush, recalibrates, slows. Crosses Wharf Street, journeys north. The last building houses a fish-and-chips place and some fancy restaurant Andrew has never been to. The basement. *Remember what Tia wrote.* They took stairs. And yes, here on the far side of the building, a steep staircase. A wrought-iron gate at the top. He grasps the gate and shakes. Solid. No wavering hinge.

'Shit.'

He peers through the gate. At the bottom a door, brushed-steel grey and flat, no way in. A walkway tucked against the building disappears into the gloom. The landing at the bottom of the stairs is strewn with garbage, leaves, and, judging from the smell, piss. Andrew pictures the trio of drunk university boys lining up the weekend before to relieve themselves through one of the myriad glory holes in the gate.

So, mate, how does it feel having your proof?

What proof? This is nothing. I need to get down there. I need to get in.

You have it: the staircase, the door, the guy.

Which guy?

The guy who said there was a nightclub here.

You suggest I trust that guy?

He seemed to know.

Andrew turns his back to the gate. Tia's delusion takes shape. Bits and pieces of nothing cobbled together with real life, this bit of history, this very real staircase. He will go home and they will talk and they will sort this out. They can talk to the restaurant owner about getting into their basement. Then she will see it's just a storage space for tins of anchovies.

Secrets. Hiding places. Middle-of-the-night orgies.

This is not helping.

You're being an idiot. You're gonna give up 'cause your little investigation hit an obstacle?

This is not about Pacifique. She is nothing. This is about Tia.

Must go. He crosses the street, returns to Bastion Square. The man in the pageboy hat is still there.

He does not look at Andrew when he says, 'Hey, man.'

Andrew jolts. Stops.

'Some people don't want to be found.' The man stands and walks across Andrew's field of vision.

'What in hell does that mean?' His voice echoes off the cobblestones.

A bit loud, brother.

The man does not react, does not stop, is gone around the corner.

Chapter 32

The bedclothes tossed aside, a pillow at Tia's feet. She picks it up. The smell of sleep, Andrew's shampoo, his shaving cream.

'You make me promise to come back and then you're not here,' she says.

She places the pillow where it belongs, yanks on the covers, drops them. *Who cares?* She slides the closet door across Andrew's side. The tip of the blue folder peeks from underneath the bottom sweater, a hulking, dark brown thing a woman she once lived with gave her. The sweater, too big to fit under a coat, the scratching against her neck too steely to ignore, languishes in the closet. But it is a beautiful sweater and she has held on to it. Plus, it offers a perfect hiding place. Or so she thought. She snatches the folder. The story of Pacifique is gone.

The sway starts in her lower back and radiates like an orbit. She lands on the bed, reaches for the edge. Blinks away the stars that threaten her peripheral vision. The story is real. The pages, the paper. She remembers. Not imagined. Real. Taken. Stolen. *Andrew.* Her fists and teeth clench in tandem. Rage, red like a broken heart, courses through her.

'Andrew!' She screams it.

She pictures her fingers digging into his face until it bleeds, skin ruptured under her nails, eye sockets dripping under the pressure of her thumbs. She shoves her fingers into her mouth and bites, hard. Whips the hand free, grabs Andrew's pillow, throws it across the room. It hits her dresser next to the door, sends rings, receipts, a photo of her and Andrew in a heavy metal frame to the floor. The crash a beautiful orchestra she has never heard before. The silence following full, ready. She stands, sends her fist into the mirrored closet door. It pops out of the tracks, shudders like a resonating saw. Cracks of pointed light shoot through her metacarpals, merge in the hollow of her elbow, and release sparks under her healed clavicle.

She slumps onto the bed, cradling her left hand. Palpates the knuckles. Nothing broken. Her adrenals kick in, send the expected anesthetic. Her rage floats into the silent house, disappears. Quiet like a funeral. Who is dead? *Not me. Not Pacifique.*

Tia tucks her arm under her breast and pushes to her feet. She takes a notebook from her bedside table. A diary of sorts, a dream journal, a thing she has around in case. It's nice. Cream-coloured paper, heavy. A gift from Andrew. She scrabbles for a pen, finds one, closes the drawer. Glances at the bed, her hand, a phantom limb. Leaves the room.

She places the notebook on the kitchen table and sits. Her fingers won't hold the pen. She tries the right hand. No. She blows warm air into the punching hand, takes a deep breath, clasps the left with the right, stretches the fingers. Drops her head back, inhales against the pain. Puts each finger in its place. Grits her teeth when she contracts the muscles that must engage to write.

It will be a short letter.

Chapter 33

The letter on their kitchen table is the first thing he sees. It ruffles in the draft he let in, skips back, settles. He releases the door and it whooshes shut. *Andrew* at the top. The fog on the road ahead of him lifts. The path clean and clear and made for one.

Don't.

I have to. She wrote it for me.

You don't want to know what's in there.

I must know.

You can pretend you never saw it. Wait for her to come home. Words said in anger. In passion.

Perhaps.

Sit down, at least. Isn't that what they always say, for bad news?

For it is bad news. It cannot be anything but.

Andrew,

I didn't want to leave this in a letter. I came home. You weren't here. I couldn't wait. I am sorry for all I have put you through. I am sorry for the things I said. For the understanding I still couldn't give you, after all this time. I know you took my Pacifique story.

I must leave. I must find Pacifique. Please forgive me. You of all people understand that sometimes we must simply believe.

Whatever happens, know that I loved you. In this moment that I say goodbye, I love you still. May you find peace in this crazy world. Love, Tia

He searches for anger, for a string of expletives to launch at the woman who spirited away his love. It does not come.

Jesus fucking Christ.

'Oh, Tia.'

Andrew brings the page to his lips. Kisses it the way he kissed Tia on their second date. For the first date, they went for coffee, talked for hours into the evening, and after a hug goodbye, he put her on a bus to her parents' place. That night he lay in bed and imagined what Tia would look like in a wedding dress. She wore a crown of flowers he could not name. The second date, they went to the theatre attached to the psych hospital. He nodded at the patients he recognized, got blank stares back. Put as much as he could afford into the donation bucket. He and Tia laughed at the kids' movie, chosen because it was about the secret life of monsters under the bed. Pure brilliance. The system overthrown in a moment by its own moviemaking industry. Later, of course, cynicism returned. Of course it was fantasy. He and Tia loved it and howled at the inside jokes along with the other hospital alumnae and the inmates allowed to attend. He had borrowed his mother's car and drove Tia home. She reached for the door handle but did not pull. A surge of confidence shot through him and he leaned in. She dropped her hand, shifted an inch closer, two. When he met her lips, he barely touched them, confidence only enough to get him to the moment before it mattered, the smallest part of him the part that kissed her. A tiny true bit unfettered by everything that had come before and would come again. Present and very much aware. Enough electricity between those lips to light the entire seven-floor building where they had met. They pulled back at the same time, and Tia's cheeks burned plum-blossom-pink in the yellow glow cast by the street lights.

'Thank you,' she said. Her smile so shy and sweet, a solitary dimple popped up beside her chin. He had never seen it before.

He waited for her to get the front door open, and when she waved he waved back, leaning over to make sure she could see him in the dim.

And she did, she smiled that funny scrunched smile again. He knew, with perfect clarity, they were meant to be.

Oh fucking Christ, no.

Mad as a hatter.

She is.

Didn't see that coming.

Me neither.

You've gotta do something, mate. You can't let her off her-fucking-self. Think, think, think.

I have time. I was not gone long. Pills? No, no.

It has to be …

… special.

Not just any suicide.

A suicide that'll get her back.

An accident.

Her bike.

Andrew runs.

Chapter 34

The bike in its highest gear, yellow lines on asphalt disappearing like frames of a film reel. The bite in the air evaporates when it meets her skin. Quadriceps and hamstrings contract, extend, contract, extend. A rhythm echoed by the wheels' whoosh, the steady beat of her heart. Damp late-afternoon breeze chills her nostrils; when it hits her lungs, it's hot, fire for the journey. Faster. She rides south on Cook Street. She takes the bike lane, flies past meandering cars. She doesn't stop for pedestrians. Sometimes your journey takes you in a straight shot. She will follow this true, plumb line to the end. The beginning. Five hundred metres ahead of her is the ocean. To get there, a cliff, a drop.

Dallas Road appears. She fights the instinct to slow. A second, stronger power, adrenaline, kicks in. Fight and flight together when it matters most. Cars zoom from east and west into and out of her peripheral vision. She focuses on the T-intersection, the curb, the stretch of grass, overgrown shrubbery. Once a fence grew in those bushes, but now there's simply a warning sign. *Danger: Steep Drop. Keep Off.* Once the sun rises higher, hang-gliders will be jumping from those cliffs.

The brain is a computer. The most powerful supercomputer. In those fractions of seconds it takes Tia to cross the point of no return at the intersection, she knows she will make it. One car cruises west, at least ten kilometres an hour over the speed limit. A *thank you* in the back of her mind. The SUV coming from the west, slowing for a left turn, *sorry guy you'll have to wait*, the shriek of good tires on pavement the sound of a thousand frightened gasps. The driver veers left, and Tia rises off her seat, pumps her brakes, and hops the curb. She stands on the pedals, seeking to regain the momentum she lost, up, down, harder, almost there, and Pacifique rises from sitting, hidden in the tall grass. Tia brakes, hard, the wheels skidding on the soft earth. The familiar teetering of centre-of-gravity losing itself. She releases her front brake a smidge, clamps on the rear. Pacifique steps into her path and catches Tia as she tumbles off the bike that just won't stop. Grabs her in those lithe, strong arms, steps back two feet, pulling. They both turn and watch the beautiful green bicycle careen over the cliff.

Silence. The bike hits the beach. Something flies off into the drift-wood. Tia expects the bicycle to bounce. Instead it lands and stops, still. Tia a body with no limbs, everything but her torso numb. The hands clutching Pacifique's arms shake, the chest in her jacket rises and falls, rapid. All is silent. Pacifique relaxes, turns Tia in her arms, faces her. Her hair is cut in a pageboy bob, slanted razor-sharp bang across the brow. Straight and lustrous, brilliant. Everything else about the face is the same: clear, glowing skin; orange freckles like stars across the nose; black brows riding Pacifique's supraorbital margin like comets. Amaranthine, it comes to her then. The eyes, the same colour as the flower of the amaranth plant, which her mother used to grow when Tia was a child. Yvonne would gather the seeds and pop them in a hot pan for breakfast.

'Your bike,' Tia says.

'*Your* bike,' Pacifique responds.

Blood shoots into Tia's hands and her grip on Pacifique's arm relaxes. That voice. Her voice.

'What the hell were you doing, anyway?' Her eyes brim. 'Not much point in me coming back if you're a corpse.'

'You came back?'

'I'm right here, aren't I?'

'You came back for me.'

'I did.'

'And you left me.'

'I did.'

'Why?'

'Kiss me.'

'That's not an ans– '

Pacifique stops her with her own mouth, and she lets the words fall away, and in the kiss there is everything that ever was, two little girls, best friends, before romance could ever play a part, before Tia knew her own heart would tell her it was okay to open for a woman. Pacifique's lips feel like they did, but there's a clarity about the kiss Tia doesn't remember. The rush of the ocean and a motorcycle's unmufflered roar their own private background music. Tia's neck protests at the angle. She bends at the knee, wraps her still-buzzing arms around her lover, and lifts. Pacifique exits the kiss to squeal like an eight-year-old. Tia gathers force, hands cradling Pacifique at the place where ribs meet vertebrae, and spins her.

'I remember this,' Pacifique cries, her bob bouncing each time Tia puts metacarpal to grass, the turn a merry-go-round she could ride forever. 'You used to do this with me when we were little.'

Pacifique older by a couple of years but even then smaller than Tia. Skin and bones, chest that she bemoaned would never grow into breasts, the mad mane of ringlets the only voluminous thing on her. When Pacifique showed up – at Tia's school or in the middle of the night at the window – she liked to jump into Tia's arms, wrap her monkey legs around Tia's waist. Tia would twist, a weather vane spiralling in the wind.

'I remember,' Tia says.

Pacifique's face is open, is void of any sadness or holding back, of the mystery she carried with her those five days in February. Forgiving.

'I remember.'

Epilogue

Tia's metallic green bike is not in the rack next to the apartment building. Andrew slows for the gate, throws it wide, veers south. At the end of the block, he takes a left. His lungs burn already. He cannot remember the last time he ran, really ran. His heart pumps a chaotic rhythm. Above that discomfort, a stronger pressure, a lightness. He slows to turn right at Cook Street and gathers more speed as he heads south to the ocean.

He catches the eye of someone familiar, a neighbour maybe, the woman who works the till five nights a week at the grocery store, the liquor store lady, no one, he does not know. Her face dissolves into strangeness. Monsters sent to steer him off course. He will not comply. He breaks eye contact, returns his focus to the sidewalk ahead of him. Three more blocks. Faster. Ahead he sees the intersection he will cross, the break he knows, the fall he imagines. Nothing. He sees nothing. Two blocks. The scene is not right. Too right. Everything is right, normal, as it should be. Where are the sirens? The crowd of onlookers? The woman being restrained before being belted to a stretcher, pulled into an ambulance? Carry her away to somewhere safe, lock her up, she is a threat to herself or others. One block. There is a couple walking their dog along the escarpment. They pass the spot she would have gone over, look, yes, do they see it?, no, just a glance, carry on. Nothing. He screeches to a halt, his knee locking, his pelvis going forward, a jolt of discord echoing up his leg. The car's horn yaws past, muted, otherworldly. Look right, nothing, run, run, run. Tire tracks. A second set. Did they go together? He skids to a stop before the ground gives way, leans over, feels gravity pulling at his belt, *come, come over*, no, *Jesus Christ, mate, what the fuck are you doing?* He pinwheels. *For fuck's sake.* No, this is not his jump to make.

Breathe, mate.

One breath in, one breath out. He steps back and leans over again. No cracked skull, no blond hair splayed like a lover on a bed of sand, no blood. No one. The bike! Yes, her bike, off to the left, leaning against the railing of the stairwell that goes from the beach to the street above. He runs. Too fucking far. Running on this soft earth slower, giving way with every step. He grasps the metal railing, swings himself around, takes the stairs two and then three at a time. Jumps to the landing, continues. Watching her bike. The bike. A bike. A green bike. He lands on the rocky beach, grabs the handlebars. A slight sheen to the paint, but it is chipping in places. The crankshaft needs oiling, reddish tint of rust coming on. Pedals bare, no toe clips for strapping in Converse sneakers. *For speed,* Tia said. The tape around the handles a peeling white, not a clean, fresh black.

What in the fuck?

I do not understand.

It ain't hers.

I know.

He looks up. Yes, this is the bike he spotted from the escarpment. He missed her. She is lying somewhere hidden, and that is why no one came. He lets the bike fall against the railing. Running on sand the worst, one step forward, two steps back, the endless journey just to get twenty-five metres up the beach. No one. No body hidden in a crevasse of drift-wood, no one hidden in the underbrush close to the cliff's side.

A woman laughs behind him. He spins. There she is, in the water, with … who? A much smaller woman, with short dark hair. Tia wears a sweatshirt and blue jeans. Rolled at the ankles, her feet hidden in the surf. She holds hands with the smaller woman, who wears tartan tights, also rolled up, under a skin-tight black miniskirt. Gold bomber jacket. Who laughed? Tia or the other woman?

Is that Pacifique?

Nah, she has long hair.

What the fuck is Tia doing with some other woman at the beach?

Maybe it is Pacifique.

Tia turns to the stranger, and something about her profile, the nose, the smile, does not sit right. He takes a step, then another. They do not see him. Are wrapped in each other and the Pacific spreading out ahead of them, the Olympic Mountains an indistinct coda. Closer. He does not recognize the sweatshirt Tia wears. Does not remember Tia's butt filling out a pair of jeans quite like that. He stumbles. Under his foot, a Converse sneaker. He snaps back to the pair, opens his mouth. The blond turns. She is gorgeous, golden hair brushing her shoulders, face bright and like the clear sky above them. Under the unfamiliar hoodie the woman has an undeniable hourglass shape. She sees him, for a moment, and then looks away. He wills the other woman to turn. Stares. Wishes.

Turn around, Pacifique. Turn around.

She does not. Instead, she wraps her arm around the blond woman's midsection and pulls. They step further into the waves until the water reaches knee height and when they lean in to kiss, Andrew turns away.

He retraces the steps he took to the scene of an imagined accident. He shoves his hand into his pocket and removes the letter. Flattens the creases.

Goodbye, she said.

Goodbye.

Acknowledgements

This book was written over many years in many places. Thus I acknowledge the traditional owners of the lands I occupied as a visiting white settler while I wrote. This includes especially the ləkʷəŋən and W̱SÁNEĆ peoples and the Songhees and Esquimalt Nations, on whose lands the novel is set, and the traditional keepers of Te Awa Kairangi, on whose banks I now reside.

Many individuals contributed to this book; the names below form only a partial list. Please forgive me and my frail human memory if I have forgotten you.

Pacifique the manuscript wouldn't exist without the mentorship and care of Dave Margoshes. Thank you.

Pacifique the book wouldn't exist without Amanda Leduc. Thank you for championing this work, for your generous and astute edits, and for your friendship. May I live long enough to properly express my gratitude.

Natalie Olsen, thank you for the cover. I remain astonished.

Thank you to the Coach House Books team, especially Alana Wilcox, Crystal Sikma, James Lindsay, Lindsay Yates, Tali Voron, and Sasha Tate-Howarth. Thank you also to Cassie Smyth, Mich Anger, and Stuart Ross.

For your generous words, my deepest thanks to Alicia Elliott, Adam Pottle, and Debbie Willis.

Sara Peters, you transformed my understanding of the manuscript. Rilla Friesen, you brought *Pacifique* into submittable shape. Thank you also to Terry Jordan and Tina Shaw for your readings.

I am also grateful for Canada Council for the Arts funding. To Tish at d'Lish, thank you for the peanut butter cookies, which fuelled much of the writing of this novel.

To my MFA colleagues who saw *Pacifique* grow, especially Elise Marcella Godfrey and dee Hobsbawn-Smith, thank you. And thank you to my teachers and thesis committee members at the University of

Saskatchewan: Joan Borsa, Hilary Clark, Erika Dyck, Kathleen James-Cavan, and Guy Vanderhaeghe. Thank you especially to Jeanette Lynes, whose faith in this novel never wavered.

To my teachers John Gould and Lorna Jackson at the University of Victoria, thank you for supporting my early short fiction. To Bill Gaston and Devin Krukoff, who looked at early versions of this novel, thank you.

To Paul Millar for the idea, thank you. (Alex, for the original title, thank you.) For being there when the title became real, thank you Ashley Little.

To ngā wāhine o Te Herenga Waka, especially Sally Day, Anahera Gildea, Alice Little, Jenny Tomscha, Lizzie Towl, Jessica Wilson, and Sarah Young: kia ora for your support while I was editing *Pacifique* and trying to be a PhD candidate.

Tyler Balone, Marilyn Biderman, Eli Bovard, Jamie Broadhurst, John Brown Spiers, Jessica Bruhn, Marjorie Celona, Yolande Cole, Gabe Davidson, Ben Egerton, Stephen Harrison, Alicia Irwin, Fiona Jager, Ebony Lamb, Fionncara MacEoin, Michelle Meier, Anna Moore, Arwyn Moore, Chelsea Rushton, Artur Shashlov, the Swedish couple at the vegetarian café in Inverness, Greg Urantowka, and Alejandro Valbuena, thank you for reading, supporting, listening, and sharing.

Much of the psychiatry and mental health 'treatment' I've encountered has been harmful, as it is harmful for many survivors; however, I have met some bright lights. Thank you, Tricia Best, Bella French, Claire Miranda, Beth Moore, and James Sacamano. To the mad activists and survivors who came before me, my gratitude goes out to you.

Thank you, Mom, Michael, Xiaoling, Max, and Molly. I love you.

Finally, thank you, Ravin and Bagel. Ravin, this book is possible because of you.

Sarah L. Taggart is a queer writer with lived experience of madness and forced psychiatrization. She has published short fiction in *The Malahat Review*, *The Fiddlehead*, and *Journey Prize Stories*. Her short fiction won the Jack Hodgins Founders' Award for Fiction and was an honourable mention in *The Fiddlehead*'s annual fiction contest. She lives in Pito-one, near Te Whanganui-a-Tara, Aotearoa New Zealand with her partner and their dog, Bagel, and is pursuing a PhD at the International Institute of Modern Letters, Te Herenga Waka–Victoria University of Wellington.

Typeset in Arno Pro and Picket.

Printed at the Coach House on bpNichol Lane in Toronto, Ontario, on Zephyr Antique Laid paper, which was manufactured, acid-free, in Saint-Jérôme, Quebec, from second-growth forests. This book was printed with vegetable-based ink on a 1973 Heidelberg KORD offset litho press. Its pages were folded on a Baumfolder, gathered by hand, bound on a Sulby Auto-Minabinda, and trimmed on a Polar single-knife cutter.

Coach House is on the traditional territory of many nations, including the Mississaugas of the Credit, the Anishnabeg, the Chippewa, the Haudenosaunee, and the Wendat peoples, and is now home to many diverse First Nations, Inuit, and Métis peoples. We acknowledge that Toronto is covered by Treaty 13 with the Mississaugas of the Credit. We are grateful to live and work on this land.

Edited for the press by Amanda Leduc
Cover design by Natalie Olsen, Kisscut Design
Interior design by Crystal Sikma
Author photo by Ebony Lamb

Coach House Books
80 bpNichol Lane
Toronto ON M5S 3J4
Canada

416 979 2217
800 367 6360

mail@chbooks.com
www.chbooks.com